sister patsy

by the same author

*Luggas Wood*
*The Yellow Room*
*The Wulfenite Affair*

# Sister Patsy
a novel

## s.k. johannesen

efp

Copyright © 2014, S.K.Johannesen,

All rights reserved.

Published in Canada by The Electric Ferry Press
Waterloo, Ontario
www/electricferrypress.com

Library and Archives Canada Cataloguing in Publication

Johannesen, Stanley
Sister Patsy / S.K.Johannesen

Originally published: Stratford, Ontario : Pasdeloup Press, 2003.

ISBN 978-0-9881098-2-7 (pbk.)

I. Title.

PS8569.O266S56 2014       C813'.6       C2014-900059-6

Lines of verse quoted are from the following songs:
"Redeemed," 1882, by Frances Jane Crosby, 1820–1915;
"At Calvary," 1895, by William R. Newell, 1868–1956;
"Old Time Power," 1917, by Daniel Paul Rader, 1878–1938.

Cover drawing by Virgil Burnett.

prologue

On a hot Brooklyn evening in 1939, the Holy Ghost descended on Sunset Park. He settled unseen over the bathing pool, the avenues of young plane trees and the new stone retaining walls, as the small circle of Friends from Ebenezer concluded their regular Thursday evening street meeting by the park entrance at Sixth Avenue.

Stars were already visible in a moonless sky. The lamps in the park stood each in its own circle of yellow light, marking the course of footpaths invisible in the dusk. Headlights threw tall shadows along the stone wall before diving down the long steep hill, where in the distance a movie marquee flashed its myriad bulbs, and in the harbour below, now black and deep as the sky, and out over the wide world, pin-pricks of light gleamed white, or coloured, some moving and some still.

In the darkness people were strolling under the trees, or sitting on benches, or lying on the grass, or heading home with quarts of Rheingold or Schaeffer to sit on the stoops or lie on the fire-escapes and catch the faint breath of wind from the Atlantic which spends itself here on the ridge above the harbour.

Everyone in the circle now breaking up felt a peculiar grace on this night under the trees and the iron street lamp. They lingered, watching the moths circle and bump against the frosted glass panels of the lamp, saying little, reluctant to return to their families, or to the rooms where some of them lived alone. Mary Colavito, who had a special black shoe on her crippled foot and dark hair on her upper lip, got up from the little plywood organ, stuffed her song books and sheets of music into a scuffed brown paper wallet and tied a bow in the thin brown ribbon stapled to the flap. Ragnar Sivertsen and Ole Knudsen laid the organ and the folding metal chair in the trunk of Brother Bringsrud's Plymouth, on top of the spattered drop-cloths and half filled cans of turps. Sister Agnes put her guitar in its case. There was nothing more to do, the Friends quietly dispersed, unaware of the trouble about to break over them.

The Friends were not solely responsible for the descent of the Holy Ghost on that Brooklyn night in August of 1939, in the shadow of the European war. He is not a person to be summoned according to one's needs or wishes. On the contrary, He behaves according to His own intricate and arbitrary purposes, and is governed also by principles of a magnetic and electrical character, as the Friends well understood.

They often repeated among themselves a story concerning the Holy Ghost, a story they knew to be true because it was authenticated twice by independent testimony. First at a revival at the Elim tent by an evangelist from Seattle who was missing two fingers from his right hand, and again at camp meeting by an evangelist from Wales who played the concertina while he preached, holding it above his head, or swinging it slowly around in a circle, squeezing with both hands and fingering the little buttons. The stories told by the two evangelists were identical, except for minor details. They could scarcely have cooked it up between them.

A certain man (so the story begins), a farm labourer in the prime of life, a big man, is known in the district around for his prodigious strength. It is nothing to him to lift hundred-pound sacks of grain and hold them at arm's length, or to raise the corner of a loaded hay wagon with his back. In wrestling matches, in contests of rough wit, in the arts of roguery and seduction, he is always the champion. No one can defeat him. Those who have felt the weight of his wrath or the sting of his sarcasm, or who have been cheated or betrayed, wait for revenge.

The moment comes on the hottest day of a hot Indian summer.

A company of men and boys are bringing in the harvest. (The Seattle evangelist has them in the corn. The Welshman on the threshing floor. No matter.) A boy more reckless than the others engages the hero in a contest of blasphemies. Lighthearted at first, they toss mild oaths back and forth negligently with many pauses for the exertions required by the work. The banter makes the men smile and the work easier.

The sun climbs higher in the cloudless sky. The men remove their shirts, and tie kerchiefs on their brows. The mowing (or the threshing) goes faster, as though the actions of the men were a galvanic reaction to the electricity in the hot ground amid the clicking of the grasshoppers and the fermenting of the sweet clovers and bedstraws mingled in the chaff.

The great man pulls occasionally from a jar of whisky. He becomes more reckless. The blasphemies take on an obscene colour. His opponent grows pale and at last silent.

"What's the matter? Have I shut you up, boy?" the champion sneers.

Now from the edge of the circle, another, seeing his opportunity, says in a quiet but clear voice that all can hear, "Now curse the Holy Ghost."

The work ceases. Men loosen their grip on implements. The rural Samson lifts his head and sniffs suspiciously.

Emboldened, another voice says, "Go on. Curse the Holy Ghost."

With a snigger, then a leer, and finally a laugh from the pit of Hell (as both the evangelists put it), the strong man holds his scythe (or his flail, if you follow the man from

Wales) high over his head. His eyes roll insanely round the circle.

"DAMN THE HOLY GHOST," bursts from his lips.

The evangelists themselves blanch, apologizing to God and man that this terrible sentence must be recounted. Only the dreadful duty of prophetic office could have induced them to say the words just as they were said on that day.

"DAMN THE HOLY GHOST," came again from the doomed man.

And a third time, "DAMN THE HOLY GHOST."

The echo of this third and final blasphemy, which the Scriptures say is not forgiven a man in this life or the next, has scarcely faded in the ears of the terrified company when a thunderhead boils out of the sky, a cold wind and sudden darkness descend, and from the cloud a bolt of lightning falls to earth so close to the company there is no gap between the flash and the roar, between the roar and the stench of sulphur. The like of it has never before been seen or heard in any of the country around.

When this terrible visitation has passed, the sky is as clear as it ever was. The champion lies dead, his once proud body smashed to a jelly.

Both the Seattle evangelist of the three fingers and the concertina'd Welshman used exactly that word, jelly.

This story, if it means anything, means that the Holy Ghost

descends in response to sufficient conditions, easy enough to grasp afterwards, but impossible to predict or control, conditions which in this case include not merely the provocation of blasphemy, but also the sultry weather, a large man with a piece of metal in his hand (leaning here toward the Seattle man's account), and the attractive danger of nervous male bodies covered in sweat.

The Friends understood by this mesmerizing anecdote, which, in its agricultural imagery, was very far from their experiences, that the life of man in its quotidian progress is risky business, taking place as it does in the midst of forces which are not necessarily on his side.

In apportioning causes, therefore, for the descent of the Holy Ghost on Sunset Park in 1939, we should say that the lamentations of the Friends were a conduit, a channel, a necessary if not a sufficient condition. For it is well known that the Holy Ghost, who commands all the tongues of earth, loves especially the Norwegian, and sometimes the Swedish, as is shown by the disproportionate number, world wide, of messages in prophecy and interpretation of tongues in these languages, not even excepting Brazilian Portuguese.

The presence of Mary Colavito is not a contradiction but confirms a well-known and easily demonstrated fact, namely, that the presence of a small number of Italians—one or two, no more—far from diluting the susceptibility of the Holy Ghost to the sad and lilting descant of Norwegian, applies a multiplying or leveraging factor as when the breath of sorrow moves across the desolated and lonely heart.

Among the imponderables of this night is that Sara, Sara-with-the-hat-on, no longer young but still willowy in 1939, with a gold tooth and yellow hair, sang "He Could Have Called Ten Thousand Angels," for which she was famous. During this song, moreover, Brother Bringsrud shut his eyes and lifted his hands in that attitude of holy feebleness in which Simeon is represented in the Temple. Mary Colavito wept into her organ and outdid herself, pumping furiously with her built-up shoe the little blue instrument. Finally, Sister Nathalie Thornquist delivered a message in tongues and interpretation, something the Friends ordinarily avoided in public as it gave occasion for ridicule and stumbling, but which on this night was peculiarly solemn and affecting, and accompanied by deep groans, and not a few tears.

It had perhaps too a certain bearing on the case that in 1939 the electrification of the atmosphere in the vicinity of Sunset Park was the highest it had ever been or ever would ever be again.

The Third Avenue el, suspended precariously on spidery girders, was soon to be pulled down. The Culver Line and its antique tram-like cars would shortly disappear. After the War, the trolley tracks will be torn up on Fifth Avenue all the way to Fort Hamilton and the great car barn next to Greenwood cemetery become derelict. The 39th Street trolley, that starts at the ferry terminal and goes so far no one knows where it goes, will be no more, and also the trolley on Eighth Avenue. But in 1939 all of these existed still. Not forgetting the four tracks of the BMT that ran deep under Fourth Avenue. The Sea Beach Express, unstoppable and unimaginable, roaring through the earth at all hours of the day and night, screaming and rocking in its narrow bed, bearing its burden of newspaper readers to Bensonhurst and Coney Island. The cadenced rumble of the Fourth Avenue Local winding down and starting up again on its short runs, to 45th Street, to 53rd Street, with squeals of brakes and the hiss and sigh of pneumatic doors opening and closing. Every night the scream and rumble, the squeal, the hiss and the sigh, figuring in the dreams of ten thousand sleepers.

On the night in question these electrical cars and trains jammed with passengers haul themselves up inclines, around bends, through junctions, creating showers of sparks from third rails and overhead wires crossing other overhead wires, steel wheels on steel rails, and other frictions and sources of static, natural and unnatural, pouring energy into the already charged and heated air.

And in the centre of the park, at the very highest point, sits the great Sunset Park pool, the gift of the Works Progress Administration of Franklin Delano Roosevelt.

The half moon of the children's wading pool is dark and still. The great bronze shower heads, like huge inverted braziers, as big across as platters, sleep in the night. Where, only hours before, mothers rubbed shivering limbs and licked scraped knees and elbows and hung threadbare and faded towels on the iron palings, now the wide stone benches crouch vacant between square brick pillars. At the far end lies the sixteen-foot diving pool, the high white tower with two levels of diving boards lit from below. Between the children's pool and the diving pool sprawls the vast three-foot pool, longer than it is broad, flanked on one side by the gilt-decorated splendour of the bath house and on the other by tiers of cement bleachers rising into the darkness. Lights flood the water through porthole openings set below the broad, blue-tiled edge, powerful lights that you can swim up to underwater and feel candlepower streaming through your body, making it green and translucent, like the body of a fish. In the centre sit twin copper-roofed cupolas with coloured glass panes, lit from within, jewelled in the darkness.

Waders move here and there in the vastness, walking in slow motion, their legs distorted in the greenish light and casting wavering shadows on the smooth bottom. Wet-limbed braves with narrow torsos and glistening bulges in their black trunks, climb to the forbidden pinnacles of the Captain Nemo cupolas and glide in long flat dives over the tiled aprons, barking like sea lions when they surface, hands cupped between mouth and water, with a shake and a toss of heavy dark hair. The sound mingles with the charge of chlorine and rises to the top of the bleachers, the very highest place in all of Brooklyn.

There in the darkness, in the topmost place, sits Jacqueline Mills, known to the braves as Jacky from Fort Hamilton Parkway, whom they visit, on this night as on others, one at a time in the darkness.

Jacky, flat-footed and rickety, her face acne-pitted, her black eyes and wide, crooked mouth set in a good-natured smirk, shivers, in spite of the heat, and hugs her skinny shoulders. She lifts her face as the Holy Ghost, with a gibbering ripple, caresses Jacky's body and settles over Sunset Park. He flows out through the Sixth Avenue entrance past the circle of Friends now saying goodbye to one another on the pavement next to Brother Bringsrud's Plymouth. He shambles and slides invisibly, south along the ridge by the harbour, up and down the streets on either side, seeking Sister Patsy.

act one

# 1

"I have a leading toward radio, Neen dear," said Sister Patsy, as though this were already a mooted topic.

Neen knew better than to be drawn, and continued ironing Sister Patsy's second-best lace collar, standing in the bay window of their second-floor flat. From where she stood she could look down the street to the right and see the tracks of the Third Avenue el, and beyond, by the waterfront, a square brick tower with the legend Whale Fuel Oils in peeling paint.

Sister Patsy was finishing a late breakfast of toast and coffee at their only table, which was heavy and dark and covered by a crocheted cloth that hung down on all sides.

Sister Patsy possessed abundant fair hair worn long and loose. It was a colour that was no particular colour, neither quite blonde nor quite brown. Her complexion was similarly neutral, pale, wan even, with no trace of pink. Her nose and chin were small and pointed and her cheek bones unremarkable. Her eyes, however, were large, deep violet under dark brows left unplucked, which made her seem unworldly rather than unfashionable. She had been an evangelist since 1926, when she was seventeen and began to preach in churches and camp meetings in the Potomac district. Even then she looked younger than she was, and she had early grown used to the power of surprise this gave her. This power, with others, belonged to the personality she had fashioned as Sister Patsy, a personality she kept strictly under the control of her intelligence. Sister Patsy held many heterodox views.

"Radio," said Sister Patsy, after a time, wiping an imaginary crumb of toast from the corner of her mouth and replacing the still virginal hankie in her sleeve, "I have a definite leading of the Lord to move out in this direction." As though illustrating the seat of this leading she touched her temples lightly with the tips of her fingers.

Neen drew up the corners of her mouth. Several thoughts, or rather sentences, struggled for ascendancy in her mind, driven by a more-or-less permanent state of mild panic. Neen had soft, formless features, sallow skin, a receding chin and round, dark brown eyes with no lashes. Her blackish brown hair was pulled back into a bun and parted in the middle. She believed that anything not a description of plain fact or expressible in common maxims, including any plan of action whatsoever, was crazy. She had learned not to say this too often, although it went through her mind frequently, and did so now.

"You better watch out for that Thornquist woman," Neen said.

Sister Patsy thought about this. The actual threat posed by Nathalie Thornquist she entertained only fleetingly. She was interested, however, in all of Neen's deliverances and kept her instincts sharpened by attending to Neen. What Neen thought, others would think. She decided for the moment to ignore the remark.

"On a clear day, Neen, from the top of the park, you can see The Empire State Building. Did you ever notice it? It looks wonderful there, all by itself. Such a—" Sister Patsy paused, as though much depended on the right word. "Such a lovely shape."

At this Sister Patsy got up and went to a pier glass near the window, where the light fell on her face. Instead of looking at herself she stood sideways, leaning delicately on the wall in such a position as to offer a double image of herself. The two Sister Patsys, the real one and the mirrored one, stood almost cheek to cheek, the mirrored one looking intently at Neen, who was so startled that she held the iron down too long and had to snatch it up.

"I went up there to the park the other day," Sister Patsy continued. "I stood at the very top of the hill. There is a kind of walled fort in the shape of a star, and a flag pole. You can see from there all the way into New Jersey.

"It was a hot day. You remember, Neen. There was a cooling breeze from off the ocean. And I looked across to The Empire State Building and I could see the broadcasts going out all over the city in waves right through the bricks and glass and through people's bodies.

"At that very moment a still, small voice spoke to me and said, Sister Patsy, this is the way. Walk ye in it."

"I done your things for the meeting tonight," said Neen, putting the finished collar around the neck of the dress which already hung on the back of the door. They both paused to study the effect of the creamy taupe of the collar against the ice-blue shimmer of the dress.

"The Dickey–Pottses always wears navy with peter pans the first night of a revival," Neen said.

Sister Patsy drew her satin robe closer about her and shivered ever so slightly, although the heat of the August day was beginning to penetrate the room. It came to her, as it had before, a kind of grey fog that moved sideways towards her, and a mocking voice from deep inside it that said *Run, Patsy. Run.* It came when she had momentarily forgotten something she needed to remember, like the Dickey–Pottses. It was as though a lapse, trivial enough in itself, let the defences down at her back and let the fog in. It felt as though something living, something equivocal, something not definitely either good or evil, had slipped through a crack in the cosmos. Sister Patsy fought back a panic. *Run, Patsy. Run*, it said, and it knew her name. Not Sister Patsy. Just Patsy.

## 2

Sister Patsy was born on a farm on Antietam Creek, the daughter of an unmarried, simple woman known only as Anna.

Anna lived in many different places during her uneventful life, performing kitchen and barnyard duties for her keep, handed around among the families of the Antietam congregation of the Church of the Brethren. In return for doubtful services—Anna had to be watched as one would a child—people let her sleep over their summer kitchens or in the attics of their wash houses.

In the winter she sat next to any stove where she was out of the way and made coarse quilts out of squares of dark worsteds and twills, and knotted them with red yarn. People put them on the flop bench in the kitchen, or used them for lap robes and even horse blankets. These red-knotted blankets were known as Anna's work all over the district, and came to be prized, especially after she died, of pneumonia, the year after Sister Patsy was born, and was buried in Price's churchyard, in the upper corner nearest the road to Five Forks, in a plot belonging to the last family she had lived with.

Two weeks after Sister Patsy was born—in a hen house one morning, to everyone's surprise, including Anna's—the elder Brethren gathered at Price's Meeting House, and after exchanges of holy kisses, and a discussion punctuated by long silences, decided to give the baby girl to a childless couple named Shoemaker, who lived near Roxbury, at the other end of the county. The Shoemakers had petitioned the Antietam Brethren for the care of the child, having heard about it through one of Mrs. Shoemaker's numerous kin. It weighed heavily with the Brethren that Anna did not seem to comprehend what had happened to her, and could not, in the judgment of the elders, after due inquiry among the wives of the congregation, have cared for a child. They took into consideration also that the Shoemakers were of good report, as the elders put it in their ponderous way, even though the Roxbury Brethren were some of them clean-shaven and attended camp meetings, which were unscriptural innovations.

The Shoemakers knew nothing of children, but had a great deal of experience of calves and piglets, and of generations of barn cats. When the baby was delivered safely to them, to the great relief of the Antietam Brethren, the Shoemakers made up a basket for her behind the stove and named her Patsy, after a sister of Mrs. Shoemaker's that had died in infancy.

Mrs. Shoemaker experimented with milk and whey, unsweetened and sweetened. She tried molasses and honey, and various sorts of thin mashes and gruels, dipping her little finger in these mixtures patiently, over and over again, and putting it in the little mouth to suck, night or day, on her own scheme of intervals. She judged the success of her experiments by a close study of the little creature's bowel movements. She carried the basket, with Sister Patsy in it, on her chores, setting it between the rows in her kitchen garden or wedged on the tractor between the tool box and the wheel housing when she gathered rocks out of the field or mowed the hay.

Mr. Shoemaker, who worked at the feed mill in Orrstown, besides having everything to do with their cows and pigs, a handful of sheep and the apple orchard, paid no attention. He left in the morning before first light. When the evening's chores at home were done, he sat on the back porch, his presence visible only by the glow of his cigarette, and watched the fireflies in the orchard.

The Shoemakers had a library which they never entered, this being also their best parlour. They never minded, however, if Sister Patsy did, and it was here that the growing girl went most often to be alone. She became expert at lighting a fire in the fancy gabled parlour stove, to drive out the chill and damp, and there she read or did the simple exercises in her school copy-books by the light of a kerosene lamp.

The Shoemakers never said anything about the books. It was not clear whether they had been bequeathed this treasure through some branch of Mrs. Shoemaker's family, or the books had been in the house when the Shoemakers moved into it, which was just after they married, twenty years before. Perhaps both these things were true. In any case they had evidently been the property of a clergyman. The bookplates, which were engraved with an emblem of a cross resting inside a crown, surmounted by a wreath of thorns, said in a copperplate hand, after the words Ex Libris, The Rev. C.C. Weaver.

Nor did the Shoemakers remark about Sister Patsy's reading. With no guidance, nor any prohibitions, Sister Patsy read what she liked. She had no reason to think of anything she read as either beneath her understanding or above it. Likewise, there was no one to tell her what was important and what was not, what was moral and what was doubtful or corrupting, what was factual and what was imaginary. She was guided only by her own curiosity, and constrained only by her own whims and the limits of her powers of concentration. The Shoemakers, by some rule agreed tacitly among the three of them, never called Sister Patsy away from her reading even when she missed meals or it grew past her bedtime.

Or perhaps this diffidence was only an element in the personalities of the Shoemakers. Mrs. Shoemaker was not altogether right in her mind and talked to herself, sometimes furiously, and went to sleep at odd times on a daybed below the stairs with her shoes on and her prayer cap still on her head. Mr. Shoemaker never spoke about it or called for his dinner when his wife's times were upon her.

The Rev. Weaver's library consisted of volumes of collected sermons of evangelical worthies of the past century, hymnals of a Methodist cast, camp-meeting song books with shaped notes, antique mystical writers such as John of the Cross and Madame Guyon, and modern expositors of the Deeper Life. There were concordances and handbooks on the Bible and on the customs and manners of the Hebrews and the geography of the Holy Land, the Works of Josephus, Matthew Henry's Commentary, a set of annual outlines of Sunday school lessons, and volumes of missionary reports of various evangelical denominations.

There were also sets of works by Authors, and Poets. Sister Patsy read Tolstoy and Henty, Tarkington and Scott, Haggard and Louisa May Alcott, Defoe and Charlotte Brontë, Longfellow and Mrs. Browning. And Bunyan, in a heavy volume with thick embossed covers and fearsome illustrations, over which Sister Patsy pored with intense interest.

All these things, and many others, flowed in channels worn by affinities created in an untutored mind. Alan Quatermain was assimilated to Christian, Christian to Crusoe, Crusoe to Hiawatha, all of them to Christ. Lonely, brave men, sexless, self-sufficient, knightly. All narratives were true. Every story pre-existed in the intricate patterns of the Divine Dispensations, which she misread from the crabbed and sententious footnote explanations of a big Scofield Bible that lay open on a special table of its own, and which she turned into her own theology of transformations, from Innocence to Law, from Law to Grace, from Grace to Holiness, and all resting in what she came to call the Divine Judgment, which was otherwise unknowable except as expressed in beauty. In Sister Patsy's view the Divine Judgment loved transparency and clarity over all things. The good was the same as the beautiful, and was something visible and stood in the light. Names were the same as things, yet were stronger than things. They represented things and also gave their keeper power over things. Names, more than faith, were the evidence of things not seen, the substance of things hoped for. Names brought the thing itself into the light, into a brighter light than the light of nature.

She collected leaves of trees and named them. She gave Mr. Shoemaker's pigs names. She gave names to features of the land, and names to the people who, from time to time, called at the Shoemaker's farm, the bonneted ladies and black-suited men from the Brethren, the salesmen who called, and the tramps. These were secret names, that she did not confuse with the names she was required to use outwardly. She had no dolls and would not have cared for them. She hoarded instead her collection of names, and made imaginary boxes and shelves and whole rooms for them. She ran them over in her mind, or repeated them out loud when she was alone, especially in the field or in the orchard, until they became nonsense and broke free from reference and were united with pure sensation, and truth and beauty became one, which was Christ.

# 3

The imminent arrival of the Dickey–Potts Trio meant that Neen and Sister Patsy would have to hang up sheets for privacy and organize their already cramped bathroom to make room for three more lots of soap dishes, bottles of wave set and shower caps, and string up lines for washing.

Velma Dickey was red-haired and fat and jolly, with many chins, She did all the introductions of their numbers and had a way with people that made them smile. She played the accordion and the guitar and sometimes the banjolin. When she sang she threw herself into it, shutting her eyes and flinging her head back. She sang the middle parts, which was usually the melody, in a strong clear voice that meant you could hear all the words, which was important because the Dickey–Pottses wrote some of their own verses and added them to the standard gospel and camp-meeting numbers.

Loreen Dickey was older. Thin and angular, she wore round steel glasses and had hair on her cheeks you could see if you stood close. When the trio performed, Loreen pretended to be more humourless than she really was. They worked this up into a little banter before their songs. Loreen was the manager of the group. She played the vibraphone and the Hammond organ, which were expensive and unwieldy pieces of equipment that had to be loaded and unloaded with care wherever they went. She sang a kind of watery soprano in close harmony with Velma.

The third member of the trio, Eunice Potts, was eighteen, tall and large-boned, and carried herself with the awkward grace of an adolescent boy. She had a cap of curly gingery hair and a red face with a small pug nose in the middle of it. She slept on a military camp bed that they carried with them in the bus.

Eunice had been an orphan in a home in Harrisburg, and attached herself to the Dickey sisters at a tent revival when she was fifteen and the sisters were the Singing Dickeys. They taught her to sing, which she did in a bass voice that startled people when they first heard it, and afterwards liked to listen to, as to something vaguely illicit. The sisters also played this up as part of their act, and out of a certain instinct in these matters, without actually thinking deeply about the reasons, they got the idea to buy a trombone for Eunice, and lessons for her to learn to play it. To this Eunice had added facility on the euphonium, which was her own idea, and on which she played unaccompanied solos.

Sister Patsy was already revolving in her mind the possibility of enlisting the Dickey–Potts Trio in her radio venture, which cheered her. They would have to be used with care, of course, and the advantage of radio was that they would not have to be seen. The radio station would have its own Hammond organ. Naturally she would have a theme song. "Singing I Go," or "In My Heart There Rings a Melody," with Eunice singing the melody in her bass voice, which would contrast effectively with Sister Patsy's speaking voice, and the others accompanying, perhaps humming. Then she, Sister Patsy, would say "Thank you Sister Eunice, Sister Loreen, Sister Velma," and nothing else, or perhaps only "Thank you, ladies," and not say anything about the Dickey–Potts Trio.

In the course of these musings the outer bell rang. Sister Patsy stayed where she was by the pier glass and listened as Neen went out to the landing and down the stairs to the first floor with a heavy uneven tread. Clump, *clump*, clump, *clump*. She heard the door to the vestibule open, then the heavy outer door, then the murmur of voices, then the outer door closing, which had a squeak, and the inner door closing, which had a swish, and two sets of heavy steps slowly mounting the stairs. Sister Patsy had a premonition of unpleasantness.

# 4

The highlights of the Shoemakers' summers were the four weeks of Roxbury Holiness Camp. There were cabins for rent and tents pitched in a grove of tall, slender shagbark hickories and pin oaks. The camp was built on the site of an old charcoal-burners' encampment, which made the ground everywhere around the grove dark and springy, covered with moss and bracken, stiff little blueberry plants and patches of poison ivy.

Since the Shoemakers lived near the camp they did not rent a cabin or pitch a tent, but drove over in Mr. Shoemaker's buggy, with Sister Patsy sitting upright on a bale of straw in the box behind, three miles in late summer heat through aisles of Queen Anne's lace and chicory and rocket and heavy, nodding elderberries, nearly every evening, during the weeks of camp, and usually for the entire day on Sunday. On these Sundays, the Shoemakers wandered about the grounds greeting acquaintances from previous years, or sat in an arbour in the grove where people gathered to eat and talk. They brought a picnic lunch of sandwiches of Lebanon bologna, with pickles, potato salad and plums, large fruit jars of homemade root beer, and a small one of the elderberry wine that aided Mrs. Shoemaker's digestion. Towards evening, when the iron bell announced the meeting time, the Shoemakers joined the throng moving in ragged lines on the beaten paths from the cabins and the grove of tents and the picnic arbours, toward the great tabernacle.

Sister Patsy could ever afterwards recall at will, in all its detail, this wooden cathedral, with beams overhead more intricate than a barn's, sawdust underfoot, open on all sides to the air. She could remember the last light of the day slanting in under the eaves, filtered green-gold through the cottonwood and box elder, the smell of washed cotton and washed bodies, like crushed butternut husks and sassafras, paper fans in gentle agitation in calloused, lye-soaped hands, five hundred voices raised to sing of Beulah Land and Mount Pisgah and Bringing in the Sheaves, the phrases of the camp-meeting songs and the phrases of the sermons all forever insinuated into one another, forever stuck in the amber of light and fragrance.

When Sister Patsy was thirteen her straight girl body gave way, under the calico dresses Mrs. Shoemaker cut to the pattern of Brethren women, to small signs of puberty. Sister Patsy no longer ran everywhere pell-mell, or squatted on tree limbs with her dress kirtled about her waist. She moved with self-conscious deliberation, not awkwardly, but experimentally, with economy and concentration, and a repertory of graceful gestures peculiar to her.

In the first summer after the beginning of this transformation of her body, Sister Patsy had an experience, slight enough in itself, which she afterwards understood to be the beginning of who she came to be.

The children of the Brethren at Roxbury camp meeting played in a waste ground of gritty sand out of earshot of the tabernacle. There were two sets of swings with plank seats, one low for small children, one high at which the older children pushed one another by running under and through, or stood on the seat and pumped themselves up as high as the bar itself, or twisted round, drawing the chains tighter and tighter and then unwinding and making themselves dizzy. There were also see-saws, a row of them on a single long beam, and two slides, one short and one tall with a hump in the middle. In the centre stood the monkey bars, made of pipes, forming an abstract puzzle of cubes.

The Shoemaker's Sabbaths had permitted only two diversions. Sister Patsy was allowed, after meeting and Sunday dinner, to get down from a shelf in the wash house the box with the Noah's ark and could marshal the animals, two by two, into the ark by a ramp in its side. Then, in the late afternoon, whether under the horse chestnut, or at the kitchen table with a plate of cookies, depending on the season, Mrs. Shoemaker would produce the Promise Box, which contained, printed on small cards, three hundred and sixty-five promises in the Bible. Their amusement was to take cards out, one at a time by turns, beginning with Mr. Shoemaker and ending with Sister Patsy, and read the promise on the card to the others, slowly and with emphasis. It was acknowledged among them, within the narrow bounds allotted to vainglory, that Sister Patsy excelled in this. Something about her voice, always against the grain of the usual meaning of things, musical and light in the direst warnings of death and judgment, careful and sober, fearful even, in the promises of earthly blessing and eternal life, made it as though she could see into the very secret springs of the mystery of life and death. Her readings were always followed by an extra period of silent reflection, after which Mr. Shoemaker would make a small hm-m-m and Mrs. Shoemaker a small tsk-tsk, and they would continue around again until Mr. Shoemaker sighed and put the lid back on the box.

So it was that Sister Patsy had little experience of other children. So it was, that without thinking, or perhaps preoccupied with something, Sister Patsy wandered unprepared into the playground on a Sunday afternoon, her virgin's prayer cap clean and starched, its strings lying on her white neck and throat, and looked wonderingly at the brutal geometry of the swings and slides and see-saws, and the monkey bars.

As she stood there, Sister Patsy's eye fell on a scene of pure evil.

High on the monkey bars, outlined against the declining sun, she saw a boy, her own age, not large, a handsome boy, with already maturing planes around the jaw and temples, blond hair cropped close at the sides and left long at the top and falling lankly to one side, his features nearly invisible from the light of the sun behind him. He stood in the uppermost cube, his arms folded on his chest, supporting himself by leaning forward, his thighs pressed into the topmost bar.

Below him, a thin red-haired boy was dangling into the open centre, his fingers imprisoned under the shoes of the boy above, legs uselessly treading the air and a thin wail of pain rising from his lips, a wail that cut through the squeals and shrieks of the playground. The torturer did not look down but straight at Sister Patsy, who stood apart from the other children in her own little territory of bitter sand.

"Why don't you do that to me instead?" said Sister Patsy.

Sister Patsy had not learned sarcasm, and meant that she would prefer in this instance to bear the evil directly than to be so implicated in it as she was already. She was not motivated by pity. She scarcely looked at the victim dangling in the monkey bars.

The boy did not answer.

Sister Patsy lifted a hand to shield her eyes from the sun.

"Let him go," she said.

Again no answer. Another wail came from the dangling boy.

"Your soul is in mortal danger," Sister Patsy said. These were words she had got from a book, or heard in a sermon, but in her mouth the shopworn evangelical phrase bore an unnerving prophetic quality. Sister Patsy's violet eyes and the odd poise of her young girl's body gave the words a peculiar force. The boy understood only that Sister Patsy was neither taunting nor scolding, and that this was something unprecedented.

He climbed down from the monkey bars, grinding first the weaker boy's knuckles one last time under his feet, and ran up to Sister Patsy, splay-footed through the gritty sand, arms pumping, and knocked her to the ground with a single blow of his forearm to her chest.

Sister Patsy offered no resistance. She half-sat in the sand, leaning on one elbow and contemplating the other, which was skinned.

The boy had stopped, his charge spent, his sides heaving and fists clenched. He saw her prayer cap, lying on the ground. A bit of starched white gauze in the shape of a bowl, with slender strings attached. He stamped on it and ground it into the sand and walked away past the swings, giving each a savage push as he passed.

Sister Patsy put away her prayer caps after that, and Mrs. Shoemaker did not chide her, or even question her about it. Sister Patsy also discarded a bit at a time the strict pattern of dress of Brethren women, and began to make her own clothes that were simpler and softer, with long sleeves and long waists and naturally moulded bosoms, in grey, and black, and sometimes white.

# 5

The house that Sister Patsy and Neen occupied was a faded brownstone that wasn't really a brownstone but only yellow brick. Nevertheless, it had a high stoop, and an area behind curled iron palings with a rose-of-sharon bush in the centre. A retired schoolteacher, Miss Sparrow, occupied the ground and first floors. Miss Sparrow used the ground floor entrance under the stoop, and rarely climbed any higher, so that the grander entrance at the top of the stoop was solely for the use of Sister Patsy and Neen. The stairs to their flat began just inside the vestibule door, and led up to the second floor, where a spacious landing went round from the top of the stairs to the front. Light was admitted by a tall window hung with lace curtains and a dark green roller blind. A bleached and dusty aspidistra in a glazed pot sat on a varnished stand, next to an uncomfortable wooden settee that was never sat on. At the back of the landing, right at the top of the stairs, doors led to the kitchen and the bathroom.

Toward the front of the landing, a pair of wide sliding doors opened into their sitting room, which doubled as a dining room. A similar pair of sliding doors separated this room from the bedroom. It was doubtful that they could be shut, and in any case the bedroom had no windows, being in the middle of the flat, and so it was left as a sort of alcove in the rear of their sitting room.

In the bedroom were two narrow beds with a night stand between, arranged in the centre of the back wall. There was a Bible on the night stand and a lamp that had a bulb inside a pink glass base in the shape of a shepherdess, and another bulb under the pink glass shade. The walls to either side were filled with makeshift racks and stacks of cartons that contained mostly Sister Patsy's professional wardrobe. This consisted of many similar long-sleeved dresses in white and pastel colours, a great many white shoes, and coats and hats in pastel colours and some in black.

By the time Neen and the visitor arrived at the landing and stood in front of the open sliding doors, Sister Patsy was rising from her knees before one of the dining chairs, on which lay an open Bible with limp leather covers and gold leaf on the edges. On the Bible sat a crumpled hanky. The breakfast things had disappeared.

"Do come in, dear Sister Nathalie," said Sister Patsy, turning her lovely violet eyes from an inner to an outer gaze, with becoming reluctance and faultlessly submissive grace. "Neen and I were talking about you just this morning. Weren't we, Neen?"

Sister Patsy ignored Neen's wild stare from behind their visitor. She gestured Nathalie Thornquist toward the convertible sofa on which the Dickey sisters were to be put up, but which at this moment was strewn with an assortment of velour and satin cushions and a large afghan rug made up of differently coloured crocheted squares. She herself descended weightlessly into one corner of this capacious object. Her guest, who was a top-heavy woman in a rigmarole of constricting and contradictory garments mainly yellow in colour, sank heavily into the other corner. A string of skinny golden-furred animals with black beads for eyes hung about her neck, even though it was August. She had a strong jaw and thin lips, and wore a hat with a veil, and tinted eyeglasses.

"You will forgive me," Sister Patsy offered experimentally. "These are days for prayer and fasting."

"I didn't come to eat," said Nathalie Thornquist, as though someone had offered her food.

"Ah, then you have come to devour," said Sister Patsy, deciding on the spur of the moment to skirt between playfulness and getting down to brass tacks.

"That is for Satan to do as he goes about his business, I am sure."

Sister Patsy signalled to Neen to get Nathalie Thornquist a cup of coffee.

"Neen was saying," she said, shifting tack, "what good reports there are of the street meeting at the park."

"It would be an encouragement to the others if you joined us."

"The Lord uses those instruments that are best suited to the task. It is surely a sin to regard any mere personality as indispensable," said Sister Patsy, as though something different had been suggested.

Nathalie Thornquist ignored this, regarding everything said so far as preliminary skirmish.

Her eyes had been exploring the room carefully. Now she turned them full on Sister Patsy. She did not believe there had been any fasting. She did not believe this ministry of Sister Patsy was of God. Brother Thornquist, now gone home to be with the Lord, an elder in the church but a weak man, had been one of those taken in by Sister Patsy's spiritual airs, which anyone could see were spurious. Of the flesh, if not worse.

"As you bring up the street meetings," she said, in a nasal whine which signified that she had arrived at what was on her mind, "I must tell you about a word of knowledge that came to me last night at the park. I was speaking in tongues as the Lord gave me utterance. The Holy Ghost himself descended on our little band. He spoke through me that we were truly living in the last days, and that it was coming to pass what is written about the time of the Latter Rain, when the Spirit will anoint Apostles from among His people, to prepare for the Day of the Lord."

Sister Patsy thought how little she really cared for these

people, or understood them. How tiresomely literal they were. She found herself staring, as though this would clarify things, but it didn't. She found herself also not a little frightened, and annoyed with herself for this fear. She wondered how far she could go in opposing this woman, as she felt fear give way to impatience, and regretted dissembling about the breakfast things and putting on the dumb show about fasting and prayer. She wished, vaguely, she had been more aggressive.

# 6

It was not far to Ebenezer. Left up the sidewalk to the corner, across Fourth Avenue, then a few doors further along, on the same side of the street as she and Neen had their flat.

The steep uphill walk went past the ladies' entrance of the Emerald Bar and Grill, the main entrance of which opened onto Fourth Avenue. On the opposite corner, the one nearest the church, stood the White Castle diner, open 24 hours, made of white enamel panels and plate glass windows through which you could see the hamburgers being made, and men on stools with their hats on.

On weekends there were motorcycle riders, beautiful men and women dressed in leather, who sat on their machines outside the White Castle. Neen sometimes picked up a bag of hamburgers from the White Castle for a late supper when church had gone on very long. The hamburgers cost fifteen cents, and Sister Patsy always had hers with sliced pickles and nothing else.

On the other two corners were a drug store, to which Sister Patsy sent Neen on occasion with a tightly folded slip with her intimate needs written down for the druggist to put in blue wrapping paper, and a candy store that sold newspapers from a wooden bench outside, with weights to hold down the papers and a cigar box for the coins. People bought the newspapers just before they hurried underground to the subway station in the morning and after they arrived home the same way in the evening.

Sister Patsy liked the rumble of the trains, which she felt, rather than heard, through the ground at night, especially on those nights when fog horns also sounded gently through the night in their different bass voices, bawling routinely at intervals, the steamships lined up from the Battery all the way out through the Narrows, swinging on their chains with the tide, facing first one way then the other, the aristocratic liners jumping the queue for the North River piers with tremendously deep pedal sounds, the ferries, named things like Setauket and Weehauken, weaving back and forth, from the 36th Street slip, through the line of ships to St. George or Whitehall. Each calling to the others, the sounds sometimes overlapping in their urgency like the Shoemaker's thirsty calves.

She took in everything on her walks to church. The smell past the front of the ladies' entrance of the Emerald Bar and Grill, which was the smell of old cider barrels with something sweet and dusty added, like face powder in the bottom of a handbag. The look of the sheepskin-covered motorcycle saddles like giant bicycle seats, worn smooth at the edges by the strong thighs of the beautiful men, that made her think of iron mower seats hot in the sun that burned under thin dresses. The shiny photos of scenes from films that changed every week in the showcases at the front of the Coliseum movie theatre, just two doors from the White Castle, and the flashing light bulbs on the underside of the marquee that wanted to pull you right in the door past the gum-chewing cashier. The women with stockings rolled down around their ankles and wraparound house dresses and thin hair twisted in curlers, with cigarettes pasted on their lips as they gossiped over the iron palings of the areas or from their windows, their shapeless breasts resting on crossed arms, eyes roving skeptically as they talked. The postman with his crushing leather bag and painful feet and the heavy hat that made a deep dent in his skull all around.

Two years, nearly to the day, Sister Patsy had been in Brooklyn. She had come for special meetings in an August like this one, when the polly-nose maples were dense and dark and full of wasps and dropped sticky goo on the cars, and the itchy balls of the plane trees crunched underfoot on the uneven slate pavements of the side streets.

The brethren asked her to stay and be their pastor. She had agreed on an impulse, feeling the excitement of the great city around her, although she knew nothing of being a pastor, and was appalled by confidences which she quickly forgot. She learned not only the acrid private histories of strange and repellent people but also the congregational history, which was a tedious chronicle of fissiparous compulsions.

When they had not split over doctrine, they had split over practices. There had been those who wanted their communion grape juice in a common cup, and only for members, and therefore had communion at business meetings. Some liked the body of Christ to be a loaf of crusty rye bread, with hunks torn off as it went around. Some wanted to take the elements while kneeling, not forward like the papists, but turned around in the pew, making many crumbs on the seat and drizzling grape juice on their chins. Some were against the keeping of membership lists, since they knew who they were and God knew who they were, making, as a consequence, the conduct of any sort of corporate business exquisitely difficult.

There were other divisions among the brethren. One of these had to do with whether the song books were to have the notes printed as well as the text, or only the text. Some would have Sunday schools, others regarded Sunday schools as the work of Satan. Naturally there were schisms caused by partisanship for one leader or another. Some of these went deep into the prehistory of the Brooklyn colony, in the upheavals in the history of Methodism and the Free Church in Norway in the first years of the century.

The most bitter divisions of all were over doctrinal matters having to do with the last days, the Man of Sin, the Mark of the Beast, the Signs of the Baptism in the Holy Ghost, the nature of the Spiritual Gifts and the discipline pertaining to their exercise in the church, the calling of Apostles in the latter days, and many other knotty matters in Scripture, all of which made Sister Patsy's head spin, who had no taste for such things.

The history of these arguments and counter-arguments would not nearly catch the furore, the heat and the din, the prayers in cold sweat, the fiery expostulations, the outpourings of tongues and prophecy, the desperate hermeneutics, the visions and tremblings, the setting of brother against brother, wife against husband, child against parents, the millennial hopes, the dreams of revenge, that had consumed the brethren from the beginning.

But these fires had been spent, or at least banked, when Sister Patsy was invited to Ebenezer. Exhaustion had set in, leaving only a rancorous residue in hearts, and a geography of alienation. Each storm that had passed over the community left a deposit, a small reminder of abated passions, in the form of tiny centres of activity, which, in part, reflected the fact that there were many chiefs and few Indians. Blue Cross on Seventh Avenue, which had been Siloa, a rump of the trouble-makers from Second Lutheran, was now a mission for drunks. The mission on Carroll Street met in a building left behind when Bethelship Methodist moved to Fourth Avenue, and gave the trouble-makers and disappointed lay preachers from Elim a place to go to preach to one another in a dense gloom.

Also on Seventh Avenue was Elim itself, whose members met in a former nickelodeon and who had a big tent they pitched every summer in an empty lot just around the corner from Blue Cross, and which lured many people away from Ebenezer.

Besides these places were even more fugitive and obscure meeting places. A room above a bowling alley on Fifth Avenue, an apartment somewhere in Finntown on the other side of Sunset Park next to a sauna bath, outlying semi-dormant colonies of brethren who found temporary refuge and partial anonymity in 66th Street Lutheran or 59th Street Lutheran, or in Norwegian Methodist on Seventh Avenue. Not to forget Glad Tidings in Manhattan, where the great Thomas Ball Barratt had received the Baptism in the Holy Ghost on his visit to America in 1906, and the Rock Church folk, also in Manhattan, although they were Swedes.

The regulars at Ebenezer included a core of older Norwegians who were Free Friends, united by their hatred of Elim except when there were good meetings there, which they found irresistible, especially the tent meetings, and so were most likely to be absent in the summer, and yet who nevertheless thought of Ebenezer as theirs, even though they were the ones opposed to membership lists.

Others who attended Ebenezer were Norwegian sailors who had been rescued at the missions and street meetings from drink and tobacco and such dissolution as was available in the numerous cheap boarding houses in the neighbourhood. A few authentic ex-drunks, a sort of aristocracy, became elders and preachers, men whose mild alcoholic palsies, rheumy eyes and stammers gave authenticity to their preaching and weight to their judgment.

There were recent immigrants who had young children and wanted Sunday school classes and services in English, and wanted to bring in American evangelists and singing groups such as the Dickey–Potts Trio. As did also a number of single women who worked as shop-girls and maids, who had come to Ebenezer because Sister Patsy had visited their churches in Scranton or Harrisburg, Chambersburg or Trenton, and had a crush on her, and came to the city because the mill owners at home had taken them along to be maids in Flatbush or Park Slope. They came to Ebenezer, travelling on the subways and els and streetcars, in cheap little hats, clutching the white leatherette-covered Bibles with the words of Jesus picked out in red letters that the young people back home had given them for going away, along with autograph albums they kept under their pillows and cried over at night. They taught the Sunday school classes, and made friends of the wives of the younger Norwegians, and stood up for one another when some of them married the sad Norwegian bachelors from the boarding houses. One of these was Mary Colavito.

# 7

Mary Colavito, crippled in one of her feet from birth, grew up in a noisy and violent family in Camden, New Jersey, and ran away as soon as she could to an uncle, a sign painter in Philadelphia. This sign-painter uncle was also a part-time pornographer who kept in his basement a large wooden camera and several lights on stands, with some simple props, and a darkroom, and sometimes put Mary in his pictures, and told her that they were art. Mary kept one of these pictures under the paper liner in the bottom drawer of her dresser because it was art and she was in it.

She taught herself to play the piano from a book, and played often on a battered upright with a broken player mechanism that her uncle had tuned for her and used sometimes as a prop in his pictures.

Mary's uncle treated her with kindness, and even with deference, as an unfortunate creature whom he credited with spiritual gifts. He made no objection when Mary said she was moving back to Camden.

Mary arrived back in Camden turned seventeen, and

went to live with a sister who had a small flat and said she would support Mary until she found work. Having taken some typing lessons with the small amount of money her uncle had given her, Mary found a job in a trucking company typing way-bills and figuring out the complicated rates for different sorts of goods, whether they were knocked flat, or were especially heavy, or had a lot of packing around them, so that she made herself indispensable and became the mascot of the drivers, who brought little things back for her from their travels.

She went with her sister to meetings in Cherry Hill that a Brother Albanese and his pretty wife, also named Mary, conducted in the gymnasium of a public school on Sundays and on Wednesday nights until they could build their own church. Brother Albanese's Mary could not play the piano, which was an oversight on Brother Albanese's part, but which was not held against him because he had light-coloured curly hair and a sweet bow of a mouth, and dark eyes, and a firm jaw with a stubborn beard that always showed, however much he shaved. Mary Colavito was a godsend to them. She quickly learned all the songs and the choruses and played the piano with increasing skill and with evangelical ferocity.

In the year of Mary Colavito's nineteenth birthday, Sister Patsy came for revival meetings to the Albaneses' church in Cherry Hill, and opened up in Mary's heart a space that had not existed before and Mary knew good and evil and was filled with terror.

She asked Brother Albanese if Sister Patsy would see her alone, feeling that she needed permission from someone with authority, and Brother Albanese listened, and interceded with Sister Patsy after the service. A time was set for the next day.

Mary took time off her job, which she had never done before, and set out early, walking the last ten blocks rather than riding the bus all the way, to Brother and Sister Albanese's flat above a radio repair shop, and where Sister Patsy occupied the small spare bedroom reserved for evangelists who came to Cherry Hill.

At the time arranged, Mary entered the building by a painted door at the side of the radio repair shop, and climbed the stairs to the landing. She knocked. A distant voice, clear and musical, said "Come." Mary stepped onto the linoleum of the bright little kitchen where she had been many times before to play Parcheesi and drink cocoa with the Albaneses. Beyond the kitchen she could see the bare sitting room with its second-hand green velour sofa and two matching chairs, and beyond that, two bedrooms, the doors side by side, both of them open. At the far end of the smaller of these rooms, in a small chair with open arms, by the single window, sat Sister Patsy. She motioned to Mary to approach.

The room had space only for a single metal bed, a yellow-stained plywood wardrobe, a white painted table, and the chair in which Sister Patsy was sitting. Sister Patsy wore a plain white dress with white stockings and white shoes and a pink satin sash tied around her waist. Her hair was loose and clean and floated in the yellow light from the half-pulled blind in the window at her side.

"Come sit here, Mary." Sister Patsy gestured toward the foot of the bed.

It was autumn, and cold outside, and although it was warm in the room, Mary still shivered a little. She perched stiffly on the edge of the bed where Sister Patsy had pointed, her crippled foot not quite reaching the floor.

Sister Patsy said nothing more but waited, as though it were the most natural thing to receive a visitor in a bedroom, without taking her things, or offering her coffee, or making her comfortable.

Mary snuffled, and hugged herself and rocked to and fro. She stood then, crookedly, her coat still about her, her hat now awry, and looked at the wall. She reached in the pocket of her coat with a gloved hand and took out a stiff card, about four by six inches, and handed it to Sister Patsy without looking at her.

Mary Colavito collapsed on the bed, and half lay, twisted sideways, an arm over her face, quietly sobbing.

Sister Patsy looked at the picture.

A man sits on a chair. He sits far forward and is leaning back. He wears socks and garters, and a woman's bloomers, open in the crotch, the draw-strings trailing below.

A woman, naked, is straddling him, her back to the camera, her face hidden. Her unruly hair, partly held with a black ribbon, conceals the man's face.

She is plump, folds of fat run diagonally across her back and her buttocks are high, perfectly round, very white and smooth. The camera is placed low and permits us to see her sex in the sharpest detail. A glistening cleft, like a marine creature. As much vegetable as animal, dark hair descending abundantly on either side, like Spanish moss, or like the beard of a poet, or a god.

The delicate fringes of her sex clasp the man's penis, part of which is visible above large round testicles in a smooth and nearly hairless scrotum. The penis is thick, strained taut against the angle by which it is seized, veins standing out on its surface like ivy on a young beech tree in winter.

At the side of the woman stands Mary Colavito, slight and dark, a serious and compressed face below a narrow monkey brow, looking downward, directly at the camera, an arrangement of leaves on her head, a white Grecian shift covering her from her breasts to her hips. Her legs and feet are bare and her deformed foot on its wasted leg is raised on a low stool, in white relief against the darkest part of the background. Her hand rests delicately, without weight, on the woman's near buttock, her thumb and middle finger together in a mysterious gesture of benediction, or perhaps of creative power.

This hand, its attitude and placement, more than anything else in the tableau, governs its mood, which is suspended motion, the figures moulded as though in wax, yet not dead or frozen, but glowing from within with nerveless vitality.

Sister Patsy got up from her chair and placed the photograph on the white table, face up, in the exact centre of the table, as though this placement were important. She turned to Mary Colavito on the bed, now quiet, still half lying, her legs dangling over the edge. Then she loosened the hair pins that held Mary's crushed hat, and put the hat on the far side of the narrow bed. She lifted Mary's legs, with the black laced-up boots still on, the normal one and the one built up because of her foot, and laid them carefully on the white candlewick coverlet. Then she pulled her chair alongside the bed and sat in it again and took the glove off the hand that wasn't covering Mary's face, and held the hand in both of her own, and after a long interval began to speak softly.

# 8

"Where I grew up," Sister Patsy began, "in a place far from here, there were many pigs. Long narrow ones with pink ears and white hair on their backs. I gave names to them, from the Bible. There were Bathsheba, of course, and Sapphira, and Deborah, and Rebecca, and the boy pigs were mostly kings. Two of these I especially loved. They were kept in a separate pen, and Mr. Shoemaker was particular that they had shade for the hottest days, and a bit of mud to roll in but not too much, and a place that was dry, with straw, to lie down in.

"I called one of them Jeroboam, for he had a crafty and rebellious nature and loved the mud and rolled his eye in a dangerous way, which made me think of that king of Israel who loved the high places. While the other one, whom I named Rehoboam, had a sweeter nature, and kept himself clean, and was trusting, and made me think of God's promise to save Judah, for the sake of King David, the sweet singer of Israel. I also remembered that King Rehoboam, although he was not as wise as his father Solomon, was descended from Ruth, who gleaned in the fields with Naomi and lay at the feet of Boaz.

"One day Rehoboam died. Mrs. Shoemaker thought we shouldn't leave him in the pen, because Jeroboam would eat him and perhaps also become sick and die. She said it couldn't wait for Mr. Shoemaker to come home.

"She backed the tractor up to the pen, and we tied a rope around Rehoboam's feet and the other end around the bar on the back of the tractor, and she dragged Rehoboam through a gate into a field of stubble, and I walked behind.

"We went through that field and into another that was a meadow but there were no sheep or cows in it at that time of year. At the far end of the field there were rocks, white, rounded rocks that looked like sheep themselves, and at one place the rocks rose into a little hill with a thicket of honey locusts at the top, which are covered with the longest thorns you've ever seen, even all around the trunks. And around behind the thicket was a bare patch of dirt among the rocks that had been dug up by woodchucks, or maybe a dog that was after them, because there was a very large hole that went into the hill under the honey locusts.

"We put Rehoboam in the hole as best we could, which was only part way in. But he was concealed from every direction except the sky, because of the rocks and the honey locusts, and a fence with a line of willows on the other side."

As Sister Patsy told her story, the arm that covered Mary's face relaxed a bit at a time, uncovering first one ear, and then one eye. She was silent, and listening intently. Sister Patsy paused, shifted herself in her chair, and continued.

"That night we told Mr. Shoemaker what we did, and he sighed and scratched his ear, and went out on the porch, the way he always did.

"After that I went over toward the hill nearly every day. I peeked whenever I dared. At first it was just flies, and Rehoboam swelled up so his feet stuck out. Then after about three days it stunk so bad all around the hill I had to hold my nose tight, and then it got even worse and I had to hold my breath and could only run up to take a peek and run away again. The crows and the buzzards came. You could see them circling high in the air, and they would get closer and closer, and disappear behind the honey locusts. If I got too close they would flap their wings and rise up a bit, and squawk. And at night there were the skunks. There was an extra smell in the morning that meant they had been there.

"After a week of this, the stink died down, and the birds went away. I went over to have a good look. Rehoboam was mostly yellow bones and patches of skin, some of it still with the hair on, and the skull and the backbone were picked but not completely, and there were maggots in them.

"I ran down by the fence and found a stick and some willow branches, and I pushed what was left of Rehoboam a little further into the hole, and swished the branches around in the dirt to hide that the birds and the skunks had been there and to make it all clean. Then I moved a flat rock that was nearby that wasn't too heavy and partly covered the hole with it and laid the branches I had over that. It was like a little grave. The Church of the Brethren that I was raised with didn't think that animals had souls and never thought to pray for them, and so I didn't either, but I sang a song for Rehoboam that was one of our old songs in German that I didn't understand, but it was slow and mournful.

"I didn't return to Rehoboam's grave for a while. I waited until a Sunday morning a week or two later, and was up before Mr. and Mrs. Shoemaker. I had my Sunday dress on, and best shoes, but I pulled some old galoshes of Mrs. Shoemaker's over them, and raced over the fields to have a look. I pulled back the branches, which were wilted now, and I could see over the top of the stone I had put there, and shielded my eyes and waited until I could see properly into the dark hole.

"Rehoboam was gone. Just as I knew he would be. I looked some more and squinted, to be absolutely sure. I sniffed in the hole and there was nothing but a dry smell, like root vegetables kept in a cellar for the winter, or the smell of caterpillars when you keep them in a coffee can. It was as though he had never been there. I ran home and started breakfast for Mr. and Mrs. Shoemaker, and pretended nothing had happened."

Sister Patsy shifted again, and looked at the yellow-stained wardrobe. "That was the only thing I ever kept from them."

"Why did you keep it from them?" said Mary Colavito in a muffled voice, in spite of herself.

The sun had been sinking and now shone into the room below the blind and threw a mantle of liquid gold over the two women.

"Because—"

Sister Patsy thought for a moment.

"Because that belonged to me. I wasn't hurting them by not telling them. I would have hurt myself a lot if I had. Rehoboam wouldn't have come to me again."

"He came to you?" Mary had now turned her face full on Sister Patsy.

"Oh, yes," said Sister Patsy.

"He was a king, you see. Whenever I saw him he had on a red coat, with gold braid and buttons, very proud, but sad in his eyes, because he remembered everything. He remembered that he had died, and he remembered the vultures and the other animals that tore at his body and left him nothing but rotting skin.

"But not any more," said Sister Patsy after a sigh. "I don't see him now. He has gone for good."

Sister Patsy helped Mary to her feet and wiped her eyes and helped her blow her nose into the hanky which she took from her sash, and collected Mary's hat and gloves. Then she got the photograph from the table and put it in Mary's pocket and kissed her face tenderly..

"Do not give up anything of yourself until you know what it has to teach you," Sister Patsy said.

Shortly after these events in Camden, Sister Patsy went to Brooklyn. The next year Mary Colavito rang, having asked her landlady to let her use the phone. Her landlady agreed, on the condition that Mary get the operator to ring her back with the charges. When she got Sister Patsy on the phone, the landlady listening in to see she was not cheated, Mary said she wanted to come to New York. Sister Patsy said she could use a good pianist to help in the church. And that was that. Mary said goodbye to Brother and Sister Albanese and to her sister, and packed her few things.

They had a party for her at the shipping office, and the boss wrote a note for her to give to the boss of another shipping company in Brooklyn, telling him to give Mary a job and to look out for her. When the time came to leave, one of the drivers going to New England took her in the cab with him and said he would drop her off safe and sound, which he did, and they chatted and laughed all the way to New York, through the Holland Tunnel and over the Manhattan Bridge and up Flatbush Avenue to Fourth Avenue and right to the door of Ebenezer.

# 9

"Here comes the Dickey–Pottses!" interrupted Neen, who had retreated to the landing during the interview with Nathalie Thornquist and was looking out the window by the dusty aspidistra.

Sister Patsy got up, not forgetting to give Nathalie Thornquist's hat a cool and insolent inspection, and went over to the window in the sitting room.

A roar came from the street below. Smoke streamed from the tailpipe of a red and cream bus with a tarred roof attempting to park on the steep roadway. While Neen in one window worried and bit her hand, and Sister Patsy in another smiled, the bus hit the bumper of the car behind. Engine racing, the bus next rammed the car in front, before coming to rest with a last cough.

The double hinged door opened abruptly and spilled out the two Dickeys and Eunice Potts and an assortment of valises and bags. There was an altercation between the two Dickeys about the driving. Loreen pointed at the front wheels and Velma, who had been the driver, shrugged, her eyes scanning the windows of the house. She spied Neen and Sister Patsy and waved furiously. She hit Loreen on the shoulder, pointing for her to look, and made a rush for the front door, leaving her sister to fume, and to help Eunice, who had disappeared inside the bus for more bags.

Eventually the women got themselves into the sitting room, with all their things inside and strewn about the landing, some of the suitcases already opened and changes of clothing pulled about.

"You must be hot and tired," said Sister Patsy.

"Thirsty, more like," said Loreen Dickey.

"Oh, yes, Praise the Lord," said Velma Dickey, her chins wobbling, "I could do with a big glass of ice tea. Isn't that right, little sister?" looking over at Eunice, who had sprawled, her knees wide apart, onto the settee next to Nathalie Thornquist. "You go on now and help Neen with it. Strong, now. Lots of lemon and lots of sugar. Praise the Lord."

"It is a miracle of the Lord that we got here," said Loreen darkly, taking Eunice's place on the settee, as Eunice got up to go with Neen to the kitchen, and Sister Patsy followed them to see if she could help.

"Oh, thank the Lord, He used us mightily for His Name's sake, Sister Shoemaker." Velma shouted so Sister Patsy could hear in the kitchen.

"We was in Stroudsburg last night, wasn't we, Loreen?"

As she talked Velma unbuttoned the mechanic's coveralls

she was wearing, slipped them off her shoulders, and wiggled them down over her hips with a grunt.

"Yes, we was," said Velma, answering her own question.

"At that motel. Praise the Lord. There was this woman behind the counter. And I could see that she had no satisfaction in her life, and I spoke to her about the Lord. And you know the seed fell on good ground, because she'd been raised by Christian folks, she said, and backslid. Praise the Lord."

Velma, by now clad only in an immense brassiere and underpants, tugged at a blue skirt and blouse from an open suitcase.

"Well, I spoke to that woman out of my heart," said Velma, looking critically at the creases in these garments while she spoke, "and gave her my testimony, and the tears began coming down her cheeks, and she said the next day she would take out the cigarette machine from that motel. Praise the Lord."

"No need to shout, Sister Dickey," said Sister Patsy, who had returned from the kitchen, "I'm right behind you."

Sister Patsy intended to pay some attention to Nathalie Thornquist, but she had disappeared.

"Where is Sister Thornquist?" she asked, raising her eyebrows and bobbing her head in the direction of the bathroom.

"No, I don't think she went in there," Velma whispered, in a parody of Sister Patsy's quiet urgency, and looked around as though the woman might re-materialize. "She was just here—"

They heard the door below click shut. Sister Patsy ran to the window in time to see Nathalie Thornquist's hat swiftly descending the front steps.

"Now you've done it," said Sister Patsy, and shook her head ruefully at Velma Dickey's pink knees.

Velma followed Sister Patsy's glance and looked down at herself.

Velma Dickey laughed so hard that Neen and Eunice Potts in the kitchen came running to see what was so funny. Loreen Dickey permitted herself a lopsided smile.

*Run, Patsy. Run.* Sister Patsy heard the voice close this time. Closer than ever.

act two

# 1

Nearly two years after the events in the Roxbury Holiness Camp playground, Sister Patsy went to Pentecostal tent meetings in Orrstown, at which a Brother and Sister Clutterbuck from Hagerstown were evangelists. Brother Clutterbuck was tall and gaunt with reddish hair that stood up in front, and an Adam's apple. He employed in his preaching a great painted canvas called The Chart of the Ages on which was depicted the events of the last times with lurid representations of the Man of Sin and the Whore of Babylon and the devil shackled for a thousand years.

Sister Clutterbuck was small and dark, with a large bust and large hips, and walked with a heavy foot and a forward cant as though breasting waves. She played the piano with many flourishes, stretching her right hand to do octave scales on the high keys, which made people smile and launch with abandon into the refrains of their favourite gospel songs. Sister Clutterbuck knew exactly the right moment, as Brother Clutterbuck was finishing one of his sermons, and was about to make an appeal to people to come down to the front, to get up from her place and go to the piano and play softly such altar-call numbers as "Just As I Am," or "Almost Persuaded," if the call was to get saved, or "Spirit, Now Melt and Move," if it was to get the Baptism in the Holy Ghost, none of which escaped the attention of Sister Patsy, who grasped that Sister Clutterbuck had a great deal to teach her.

By the end of the Clutterbucks' one week campaign in Orrstown they had agreed to take Sister Patsy along to help out with the song books and such things, in exchange for room and board, provided from the free-will offerings they took in.

When Sister Patsy told the Shoemakers, the night before she was to leave with the Clutterbucks, Mr. Shoemaker went out on the porch and lit a cigarette, while Mrs. Shoemaker got down a cardboard suitcase and put Sister Patsy's few clothes in it and told Sister Patsy that it had been a miracle that they, who had had no children of their own, had been sent Sister Patsy. The Lord gives and the Lord takes away, but they would always think of her as theirs, and would she think of them sometimes. This was as much as Mrs. Shoemaker had ever said to anyone at one time and it exhausted her and so she went and lay down under the stairs and was still there when Sister Patsy got up early in the morning and went out with her suitcase to meet the Clutterbucks' car at the end of the lane, taking care that the screen door didn't slam.

Over the next year, the Clutterbucks, with Sister Patsy along, conducted revivals, missionary conventions, district meetings, tent meetings, camp meetings and youth rallies. During two months in the winter they got as far afield as Henderson in East Texas, and worked their way back along the Gulf and northwards again, preaching in Biloxi and Meridian, and then in Eutaw mostly to Negroes. Brother Clutterbuck preached from his painted canvas chart, although the Negroes didn't care for it, not knowing who Mussolini was, which spoiled the impact of the revelation that he was the Antichrist, a line that Brother Clutterbuck had adopted to great effect elsewhere. They rested after that for a time in Hagerstown where the Clutterbucks had a small house that had belonged to Sister Clutterbuck's parents, in the middle of a field on a dirt road outside of town, before the season of revivals began again in the Potomac district.

Sister Patsy was not much interested in these prophetic sermons of Brother Clutterbuck's. She was frightened by the Negroes, and repulsed by the sweaty white farmers and their haggard wives. But she loved the days in the back seat of the roomy saloon car with all their clothes and song books and The Chart of the Ages lashed on top, and banners tied on either side that said Clutterbuck Evangelistic Team, rolling along dusty roads, sometimes late into the night. Sister Patsy also liked it when they pulled up at a place and the preacher's wife came out and made a fuss over her and Sister Clutterbuck and got them settled in, while Brother Clutterbuck and the preacher said Praise the Lord to one another several times and walked around the car looking appraisingly at what had to come off. Sister Patsy never minded where they put her. It was usually on a sofa or a day bed, but sometimes a clean little wallpapered room all to herself, with a ewer of sour-smelling cistern water and a washbasin on a stand and an oil lamp and a coverlet made up all over of little puckered rounds of cloth in different colours.

Sister Patsy made herself useful to Sister Clutterbuck in any way that she could, laying out her clothes, shopping for small things for her in the towns they visited. She came to see that Sister Clutterbuck was lonely and liked having Sister Patsy about. Sister Patsy watched Sister Clutterbuck closely. She learned the importance of pauses, of silence, the power of softness, of the small and the economical, things that Sister Clutterbuck did at the piano and by her gestures, the way she lowered her head, or sat when everyone else was standing, or took up her handkerchief or put it down, or touched her hair or adjusted her hem. Sister Patsy saw that the mood and direction of a meeting could be controlled in these ways, and that for Sister Clutterbuck it was just natural and came of years of being Brother Clutterbuck's wife. And he knew it too. You could see it in his eyes sometimes. He would suddenly look lost when he had made a big point or was in a delicate part of the altar call and didn't know where he was, and he would turn to her—she always sat behind him on the platform when she wasn't at the piano, and wore a corsage of waxy flowers—and something in the way she was sitting would give him the cue he needed, or just reassurance.

Sometimes Sister Clutterbuck preached, although mainly she preached to women, to the Sunday school workers at the district rallies and conventions, or at the ladies' morning Bible study in the tabernacle at camp meetings. Sister Patsy noticed that Sister Clutterbuck changed when she preached. She tried to make her voice deeper and gruffer and her chin disappeared into her neck and she looked ridiculous being short and holding a big Bible against her bosom and wearing a waxy corsage that was bigger than usual. All this Sister Patsy observed with keen interest.

It came to her gradually that she, Sister Patsy, would preach, but that it would be on her own and it would not be like the Clutterbucks.

After their rest at Hagerstown in early spring, Sister Patsy looked for opportunities, which were not easy to find, since she did not sing or play an instrument, or have a striking testimony of healing or conversion. She had always been in good health and had never sinned that she was aware of, nor did she have anything to say about Mussolini, or the Great Tribulation, or the Two Witnesses, nor any wish to bring the unsaved down to the front or see people filled with the Baptism in the Holy Ghost and speak with other tongues, which was a distasteful and sweaty business. It was not that she doubted the doctrines on which these perhaps necessary practices were based, but that they seemed far from her.

Sister Patsy was not exactly ambitious. Nor did she wish to put herself forward for the sake of doing it. She hadn't really a clear picture of where her idea would lead. Her idea was indeed limited to a feeling that something was about to happen to her, within the boundaries of this world which was now her only world.

The moment came in August of that year. Brother Clutterbuck suffered a stroke one afternoon after heaving the Chart of the Ages on to the platform of the tabernacle at Potomac Camp Meeting on the hottest afternoon of the summer and having drunk too quickly a whole pitcher of iced tea. Sister Clutterbuck brought the other ministers and evangelists to their cabin, where Brother Clutterbuck had been removed, to pray for him and anoint him with oil, although to no avail, for he never recovered the power of speech or the use of his right side.

On the day Brother Clutterbuck had his stroke, he was to have begun a week's series of sermons on prophecy in the evening at the great tabernacle at the greatest of all camp meetings in the East. People came from Baltimore and Washington, D.C., and some all the way from Philadelphia. Until now the Clutterbucks had never been given the evening services for a whole week at Potomac Camp Meeting but only led the singing and introduced the speaker, or perhaps led the Bible Study during the day at the small tabernacle.

Brother Clutterbuck's sudden incapacity created consternation among the brethren. A Brother Blubaugh was hastily appointed to take the evening service. Brother Blubaugh was fat and played the trumpet, and carried it with him to the pulpit when he preached, punctuating his sermons with fanfares and snatches of gospel songs, or sometimes just great blasts from what he was pleased to call his shofar.

While the brethren were making these arrangements among themselves outside the Clutterbuck's cabin, by whispers and many pious ejaculations and sighs, Sister Patsy spoke to Sister Clutterbuck in the kitchen over the top of the wooden icebox. When the brethren knocked on the screen door to explain their decision, Sister Clutterbuck heard them out, without opening the door, and then said it was her wish that her sister-in-the-Lord and co-worker, Sister Patsy Shoemaker, should represent the Clutterbuck Evangelistic Team on the platform tonight and say a few words before Brother Blubaugh's sermon, and if they would indulge this request she was sure the Lord would be pleased and would bless them. The brethren murmured and shuffled and nodded vigorously even before she had finished or had even well begun, so eager were they to be away from the possibility of female hysterics, saying as they went that some sisters would be by to see if there was anything she needed.

It is not certain how much Sister Clutterbuck sensed of what was to come. She afterwards said that Brother Clutterbuck, with the last words he ever managed to speak, with a supreme effort which was itself a miracle, had told her that the Lord's anointing was on Sister Patsy and that God would use her mightily. Since she, Sister Clutterbuck, was not one to boast of what had been really the Lord's doing, she would not say how they had nurtured the child and cared for her and prepared her for her ministry, and how they regarded this rôle they had played as the finest of their ministry.

## 2

The evening that followed the meeting of the brethren in the Clutterbuck's cabin is entered firmly in the folklore of Potomac Camp Meeting.

There had been a heavy shower just as the iron bell that stood in front of the cafeteria called people from their tents and cabins. They streamed from every direction towards the great tabernacle, with umbrellas and galoshes, with much good-natured jostling of one another and side-stepping of puddles on the little uneven gravel paths.

The shower had brought a quick chill to the air, so that the tabernacle, which had been roasting under the August sun, was now warmly inviting, fragrant of sawdust and the smooth dry pine of the benches. Brothers in rolled up shirt sleeves, appointed ushers and marshals, pulled down some of the canvas flaps around the edges of the tabernacle, especially on the side facing the direction of the breeze, or where they could see sisters were shivering in their thin dresses.

The choir had been warming up behind the platform in a large room that ran the width of the tabernacle, and which was also the prayer room where, after the evening meeting, seekers would storm heaven with many tears until the small hours of the morning, while specially appointed monitors kept the men separated from the women and threw coats over the legs of sisters who were slain in the Spirit.

Having finished their warm-up, choir members now filed into the rows of seats that stretched right up to the rafters at the back of the platform, behind the chairs for dignitaries, climbing up a short and narrow flight of stairs directly behind the pulpit and fanning out to their proper seats, altos and basses on the right, sopranos and tenors on the left, all dressed in white shirts and white blouses. After them came the camp meeting organist and the pianist that was to replace Sister Clutterbuck for the service, then the youth director of the camp who was known only as Brother Wayne, then the camp administrator, and then a handsome man with a boyish grin and curly hair who was the song leader and choir director. Then a confused and wispy woman who turned out to be a missionary on furlough, and finally a large woman with iron grey hair swept up and stout laced-up shoes who gave talks during the day on Christian education to the Sunday school workers. Each of these served some regular function during the service or had been invited to say a few words. They took places at the piano or the organ or moved to chairs on the furthest ends of the platform. There was then a long pause, during which time a great murmur of expectancy filled the tabernacle, not least because the news had circulated about Brother Clutterbuck, who had been removed by ambulance, wailing down the long lane to the state highway not an hour since.

When all else was in place the main platform party emerged from the little hatchway behind the pulpit, and stood there in sedate disorganization for a moment, speaking to one another as though they had not just now been together down the little flight of stairs in the prayer room, but rather had just chanced to meet here and were sorting out who was who. The crowd followed every move on the platform with open-mouthed fascination, for these were the stars of the camp meeting world. Dr. Simeon Wells, a grey little man with a crooked mouth who was the president of the Bible school conducted on the camp meeting grounds during the winter. Reverend D.D.Chase, a florid man in his sixties, vain of his snowy hair, who was the district superintendant. Familiar figures both of these, who lent gravity to things in general and theological sanction to particular points by sudden looks of keenness, in the case of Dr. Wells (who wasn't really a doctor), or, in the case of Reverend Chase, resonant Amens, produced with the merest parting of his lips and a shifting of his bottom. Brother Blubaugh held his trumpet in his left hand and his Bible in his right hand, and Sister Blubaugh, who was as large as he, in a purple dress and large purple hat, carried a trombone for when they played special numbers together, and also for when they played along with the congregational singing, giving many extra notes and flourishes to the music.

Almost lost in this company was the slender figure of Sister Patsy, whom no one spoke to.

Dr. Wells and Reverend Chase and the horn-blowing Blubaughs settled heavily on their knees before their chairs, showing their backsides to the congregation, who were transfixed by the spectacle and grew silent, as suitable intercessory moans and pleadings for the blessing of God on the evening's business arose from the kneeling quartet, Brother Blubaugh on one knee, his large hams straining against his checked trousers.

Sister Patsy remained standing for a time, her eyes fixed on the middle distance, absorbed in something, and then sank lightly to the edge of her seat, where she remained erect, her back straight and unmoving.

There were those who claimed afterwards that they had known from the beginning of the meeting that something strange and wonderful was about to happen, and that they had not been able to take their eyes off Sister Patsy. An angel, they said, so beautiful she was that night, in her simple white dress.

# 3

The meeting began properly when the curly-haired song leader bounded to the edge of the platform and announced the first song of the evening. A rattle of arpeggios from the piano. A thunderous roar of muddy chords from the organ with lots of pedal work. Then the voice of the multitude raised in an old favourite.

*Redeemed! How I love to pro-claim it.*
*Redeemed by the Blood of the Lamb.*

Toward the end the song leader held the crowd on the top notes with both hands aloft and quivering with the strain of it,

*Redee-eemed! Redee-eeeemed!*

The final words,

*His child and for-ev-er I am.*

Stretched out in the most artistic way, with a descant from the sopranos in the choir, who had been carefully rehearsed before the meeting, and the Blubaughs blowing mightily. It could not have been more satisfactory as an opening to the meeting. Dr. Wells mimed a sort of inane and giddy surprise, as though at his own cleverness. Reverend Chase passed his hand reverently over his white mane and intoned an Amen. People waved their arms about, and here and there patches of gibberish could be heard, a sort of overflow, a small release of pressure from a vast pneumatic reservoir.

So it went, the mood passing over many registers, always cooking. Through the tedious stretches of the announcements—"Will those good folks who have pitched tents in the dining hall grove please register at the camp office first thing in the morning." The reports from the mission field—"I bring you all greetings in the name of the Lord from my co-worker Brother Banerjee and the children at the orphanage." Passing out the collection plates. Taking in the offering. Waiting, waiting, for the miracle, for the dam to burst, for hearts to overflow.

In due course, following a special number from the Blubaughs, the choir filed from their places to join families and friends in the tabernacle. The missionary sister and the Christian education sister did likewise, as did the camp administrator, the song leader, the organist and the pianist (who nevertheless sat close to the front in order to slip back again for the altar call), and finally Sister Blubaugh and Dr. Wells. Reverend Chase remained on the platform in order to introduce the evening speaker, and explain about the tragic circumstances of Brother Clutterbuck and lead everyone in prayer for his recovery, and to allow Sister Patsy to say a few words. Brother Blubaugh mopped his brow and busied himself with his notes and blew spit from his trumpet, and eased himself forward in his chair in readiness.

Sister Patsy barely heard Reverend Chase explain about Brother Clutterbuck, or the murmur that accompanied the prayer for him, or the introduction of a young sister who was part of the Clutterbuck Evangelistic Team, which, only when there was an end to Reverend Chase's talking, did she realize referred to her, and so stood to her feet and walked to the edge of the platform, some distance from the pulpit.

She stood there for a long time, her arms at her side, nothing in her hands, looking at the throng of people. As she moved her head, ever so slowly, with a grace that caused all the shifting to cease, and the coughing, and even the young people outside, at the edges of the light (for night had settled on the great tabernacle), to stop their restless motions, and the fussing baby at the back to return to the nipple under the cloth laid with modest intention over the young mother's shoulder and breast, it appeared that she was searching every face in turn in this multitude, indeed as though she were looking for some one in particular. Not rejecting any one, no not that, but as though having fixed each and every one in his place and in all possible coordinates and relations, she had still capacity for another. This moment could not in truth have occupied more than a short time, but to those who were there and remembered it, time and space were swallowed in infinity. Each person was sure that her gaze had lingered on himself alone.

When she was finished her searching, Sister Patsy focused her gaze at the back of the tabernacle, as though through it and beyond it. Then she said, "Jesus."

It was said so simply, so un-rhetorically, although clearly and unmistakably, that the reaction was delayed. In the first instant it was perhaps expected she would say more, that a sentence was forthcoming, a conventional remark. When it became clear that this utterance was of another order, an entirely new use of language, an invocation of a presence, a declaration of a state of affairs, a word as a material thing, an object in itself, floating out to them and over them as though a visible rather than auditory phenomenon, there was a contagion of nervous glances, a lowering of eyes, a trembling of the muscles in the corners of mouths, a cottony rustle. Sister Patsy waited. Then, here and there, folk took on a dreamy and peaceful look. Others shut their eyes tight and rocked gently to and fro. And faintly from certain ones came soft sibilances. One murmured Jesus, then another, then several overlapping and running into one another, but subdued, faint.

"Jesus," she said again, at exactly the point that the tension was like the tension before a thunderstorm. Again there was a delay, the word arriving as an after-image rather than directly, impressing itself on the mind softer than before, and lower, the consonants prolonged, the effect sensual but not carnal, a word of welcome to a friend, a lover.

Sister Patsy had not moved her position, or raised her hands, or altered the direction of her gaze.

Now the strangest of phenomena, a species of mass hypnosis yet not exactly, rather a mass collaborative mime, a processional extension of a suggestion, as the people along the axis of Sister Patsy's gaze turned themselves inward, those on the edges craning their necks to see, and a ripple, as in a field of ripe grain, moved slowly from the back of the tabernacle to the front, Sister Patsy's eyes on the centre of this movement, whether willing it forward or following its progress no one could tell.

"Jesus," again, as the ripple broke at the front and washed back over the pine benches and the rows of people. The people emitted a low groan, yet still unable to cease their staring, not daring to break the connection with those violet eyes, that slender figure clad in white.

Then Sister Patsy said, catching the next movement of breath on its flood, "Jesus is here."

Again a breath. And another order of reality took over from the old.

Into the small prepared void, Sister Patsy said simply, "Do you smell the fragrance of Him?"

The exhalation when it came had no more groaning or agitation in it, but sweet peace. The tension went out of faces and bodies. The old looked wise and the young looked innocent. Husbands leaned toward their wives, and some put arms around their shoulders. Sweethearts entwined their fingers discreetly at their sides. Dr. Wells's crooked mouth hung open foolishly. Sister Blubaugh looked up moistly at Brother Blubaugh and ceased to hate him. On the platform Reverend Chase forgot about keeping his jaw firm and looked his age.

Sister Patsy now smiled broadly, radiantly. She said, "Say it after me." Lifting her arms as though to direct a choir of whale voices, she said quietly, her voice low and confident, riding on the delicate foam of a gentle sea, "J-e-e-z-u-z."

The wave rose, and broke at her feet. "J-e-e-e-z-u-z."

# 4

Ebenezer squatted on its site in ambiguous semi-completion, a basement for a building never built. It was begun by the Free Friends in 1911 and they eventually finished a low auditorium with wardrobes and toilets on either side of a vestibule, and a kitchen and meeting rooms at the far end, behind the platform. The thick, buttressed walls were meant to support a grand sanctuary above, for which there had been drawings, now lost, of a double entrance reached by curving steps from either side, a gallery, and JESUS! over the platform in large gold raised letters in Gothic style, exactly like the one in Filadelfia Church in Oslo. As it was, the façade, made of scored brown bricks and rising to a feeble peak in the centre, was a temporary expedient, a false front, the stout walls holding up only a flat tar-papered roof that leaked., The double door, however, was made of yellow oak, shaped to a pointed arch. A single light bulb in an enamelled metal fixture illuminated it from above, and over the pavement swung a sign in the shape of a cross that said Ebenezer down the middle and Jesus Saves across the arms.

Inside, the auditorium and the adjoining rooms sat semi-underground. Anyone entering by the front door had to descend six steps. The windows were high up and dim, and the smell of drains wafted through the building. The glum motto, No Cross No Crown, scrolled itself across the front in blue above varnished folding doors that permitted the platform to be extended into the meeting rooms behind. A round wall-clock hanging over the entrance from the street, bore the legend Redeem the Time.

The Friends frequently required the extended facility afforded by the folding doors, as most of the people who attended a meeting of the Free Friends occupied the platform. These included the piano player, anyone who played a guitar or mandolin, collectively called the string band (although like the church itself the string band had no leader and therefore did not strum together), all those who were to make announcements or offer greetings during the meeting, such as returned missionaries, with their families (although many of the missionaries were spinsters), superintendents of outlying missions, anyone at all who had been to Norway recently, and various leaders, elders and preachers, all of whom were entitled to speak, which they seldom failed to do, in long nasal harangues punctuated with shouts and foot-stamping. On very special occasions, such as missionary conventions, and when Swedish tenors came to sing, a meeting might go on all day, and row upon row of dignitaries would crowd right up to the pulpit, and stretch back beyond the folding doors and even sometimes into the kitchen. Missionaries at these special events dressed in modest and not too colourful versions of native costumes.

The baptismal tank, a dank cement hole like a garage man's grease pit, festered under the centre of the platform. The brethren uncovered it, when it was to be employed, by shifting the sacred desk, as they called the monstrous varnished pulpit, raising several square sections of the flooring by strategically placed iron rings, and stacking these squares to one side. The candidate for immersion, clad only in a night-shirt, shivered barefoot from the kitchen, navigated the string band to the cement steps, and disappeared slowly into the floor, arriving thus in front of the elder or leader—the Friends did not like the words pastor or minister—making two disembodied heads on the floor. When the baptized at last spluttered back up the steps, a sister, in the case of women, or a brother, in the case of men, stood ready at the top with a sheet to hold around their wet night-shirts for the sake of modesty and decorum, and led them back to the kitchen, leaving puddles in the string band.

Sister Patsy looked on these horrors, and made many changes. She hid the varnished doors and the No Cross No Crown motto behind a magenta plush curtain, chosen to set off her cream, or taupe, or pale blue or sometimes French blue dresses. She got rid of the pulpit, which hid her completely, and replaced it with a slender wooden stand with a little brass light, and put down a large floral carpet with a crimson background, so that she might glide gracefully to and fro when she preached and not creak on the splintery floor. She banished the string band from the platform altogether, along with the other customary platform characters, but permitted the elders to stay until it was time for her to preach.

As the result of protracted negotiations with an Orthodox Jew on Thirteenth Avenue, and a family of Italian piano movers across the street, Sister Patsy traded in the old black upright piano in the corner for a second-hand walnut-veneered baby grand with a lid that could be lifted to two different levels. Besides trading in the old piano, she made an undertaking for eighteen monthly payments of eleven dollars and eighty cents to the Jew, and a much discounted fee, counted out in coins and one-dollar bills from her own purse, with many sighs, to the piano movers, who were charmed, and waved from the stoop on hot evenings whenever she passed. On this piano she eventually installed Mary Colavito, having to unseat a Norwegian sister of no talent who joined the little band of exiles at Blue Cross, formerly Siloa.

When Sister Patsy learned about the differences of opinion about communion, she saw an opportunity to gain a reputation for wisdom and consolidate her position with both factions. Since she hadn't the slightest interest in the merits of the dispute, she was able to announce at a business meeting shortly after her arrival at Ebenezer that after much prayer and thoughtful Bible reading she had come to the view that the

Lord, ever mindful of the limits of our understanding, had not made the question of open or closed communion, Norwegian rye bread or matzoh, kneeling or sitting, cup or glass, a matter of faith, but rather of conscience and of church order. What was essential was to avoid scandal by the multiplication of fractiousness, which opened afresh the wounds of Christ and gave occasion of stumbling. Furthermore—here Sister Patsy lowered her eyes in what she hoped looked like submission to an inscrutable decree of providence—it had been opened to her that the men of the church were especially fitted by God for the distribution of the elements, and should in any case undertake it as they saw fit, but would it not be in the spirit of the ordinance that an opportunity for communion be afforded both in closed mode in the business meeting, and open mode on the first Sunday of every month?

When Sister Patsy raised her eyes from delivering her modest proposal, and looked around, she saw that Brother Bringsrud and Hans Hansen and Peter Thornquist were nodding sagely in their slow way and exchanging deep glances, and she knew that she could do anything she liked about the platform and the baptismal tank.

She had not failed to notice, however, Nathalie Thornquist's stony face behind the tinted glasses, the implacable enmity in her eyes, like the eyes of the little dead animals on her bosom.

# 5

The first opportunity to test Sister Patsy's resolve in the matter presented itself when Neen asked to be baptized in water. Or rather re-baptized, for like Sister Patsy, Neen had been brought up in the Church of the Brethren, who didn't dip just once backward, as John the Baptist is depicted doing in the Sunday school lessons, but three times forward, signifying the three Persons of the Holy Trinity. Sister Patsy could see no point in re-baptism, but it could do Neen no harm, and Sister Patsy found herself looking forward to it.

So, on a Saturday morning in late June of Sister Patsy's first full year at Ebenezer—just before the arrival of Mary Colavito—a convoy of cars set out for the camp meeting grounds in Green Lane, which was closer than the Potomac Camp and sat on a hill overlooking Perkiomen Creek, where Sister Patsy intended to baptize Neen once backwards.

Florence Hagen, who was pretty and had a tiny waist and an overbite and always wore a flower in her hair, borrowed her father's car, or took it, intending to tell him later.

Florence worked for her father in his lumber yard in a sandy waste near Plum Beach, although she hardly did any work at all, being indulged more than was good for her by her father, a silent and lugubrious widower whose generous tithes kept Ebenezer solvent. Florence Hagen ordered coffee ice cream and marshmallow sundaes when the other girls could scarcely afford cherry cokes, but she was popular with the factory girls and typists, and never took her father's big yellow Packard without packing it with picnic lunches and lemonade in a cooler, and inviting them for a spin, sometimes all the way to Stony Brook, where the Hagens had a summer house.

For the baptism she outdid herself. When she pulled up to the curb with a swish, scraping the white sidewalls, promptly at eight o'clock in front of Ebenezer, the luggage rack at the rear was stacked high with leather-fastened wicker boxes and round blue canteens tinkling suggestively of iced drinks, folded canvas deck chairs and umbrellas in red and green stripes, and a small cowboy-style guitar in a pasteboard case.

Brother Bringsrud arrived in his Plymouth, which smelt of turpentine, and there was some discussion about whether to take the portable organ and they decided against it, to uncontrollable giggles from the girls.

Sister Patsy was grateful for Brother Bringsrud, who was her main supporter among the older Norwegians at Ebenezer. The sight of his ruddy, freckled face and stiff, sandy hair, and his perpetual look of amused tolerance heartened and consoled her.

Brother Bringsrud brought two Norwegian sisters, one of whom was Sara, who always wore a hat and had gold teeth and cheek-bones like a movie star and who thought everyone looked at her, which gave her great pleasure. The other was Agnes, who was solid and played an out sized guitar with a wide embroidered strap with floral motifs on it in red and green that she had made herself. These two frequently sang together, not badly, and Sister Patsy was to think of them later as contributing to her radio program, but then rejected the idea since they promised to be impossible to manage and had, it seemed, only one tune.

Sister Sara and Sister Agnes had a little business on Fourth Avenue, although they didn't always get along and sometimes didn't speak to one another for days. The business was conducted in a tiny shop with an oilcloth-covered counter and a work table and a chipped enamel gas stove. They made fish pudding, from pounded haddock and eggs and cream and nutmeg, golden brown on top and creamy white inside. They brought some along for the picnic, to eat cold, wrapped in wax paper inside a tin from the wedding of Crown Prince Olav and Crown Princess Märtha in 1929—a treasure belonging to Sister Sara which Sister Agnes coveted. Also in tins were a lump of yellow cheese with bits of cloves in it, buttered currant buns, buttered waffles shaped like little hearts and spread with sugared wild cranberries, enough for everybody, and also bottles of fruit syrup and water, all of which was in the trunk of Brother Bringsrud's Plymouth.

Right behind Brother Bringsrud, a shiny Chevrolet coupe with a rumble seat pulled up with two bareheaded young men in shirtsleeves. The driver, Ole Knudsen, was a house painter with big creased knuckles on his thick fingers and tiny flecks of dried paint he could never quite get out of the creases or off his forearms, which were muscular and covered with fine gold hairs. There was sexual electricity between Ole and Florence Hagen that was like a smell, like the smell of the ladies' entrance at the Emerald Bar & Grill, and in which the sharp bitter smell of cold Rheingold beer was an element, although not acknowledged, because none of the Friends drank. House painters, however, were understood by the nature of their calling to develop peculiar thirsts, as they worked in fumes and heat in close quarters, sometimes with nothing on under their loosely hanging and spattered white overalls so that ladies never came around where they were working without blushing.

The factory girls and typists pulled back from Ole as from a too-hot stove.

With him was his friend Ragnar Sivertsen, who was slight, especially in the legs, and had big ears and a long jaw and pale blue eyes that twinkled sometimes as though at a private joke. Ragnar had been a sailor and then put up metal ceilings, which were going out of fashion, and now worked sometimes with Ole when there was extra work for house painters. Ragnar was getting tired of the boarding house, where he lodged with Ole and three other men, and was beginning to study the factory girls and typists with a speculative eye and a worthy but incapacitating respectfulness, not knowing how one went about such things. He spent part of his lonely evenings writing long letters to his mother in Norway in which the raffish doings of Ole, and how Ragnar was hoping Ole would reform himself in time, played a part she rather wished were reserved for encouraging news about himself. The last such news was that he had been saved at a street meeting on Hamilton Avenue, and that was nearly two years ago.

Sister Patsy noticed that his gaze rested occasionally on Neen, although Neen disdained to notice. Neen's name figured casually from time to time in Ragnar's letters. His mother in Norway, who was shrewd, in the way of mothers, tasted this name experimentally on her tongue, and gave a little shudder.

The company sorted itself out quickly. Neen got in the front of Brother Bringsrud's Plymouth with the two Norwegian sisters in the back. Sister Patsy put the two giddy factory girls in the rumble seat of Ole's coupe, and got into the front next to Ole. Ragnar was sent up to the Packard to be crushed in the back with three typists, while a fourth rode up front with Florence Hagen. And so off they went to the ferry slip at 36th Street.

After the ferry—on which they snapped pictures with a Kodak with enormously long bellows belonging to Brother Bringsrud, and which set off the factory girls and typists yet again—they drove across Manhattan to the Holland

Tunnel, and were before long rolling through New Jersey and Pennsylvania in the sunshine, their spirits lightening with the miles and the soughing of the tires on the hot tar. The little wing ventilators were turned inward, bathing them in scented air, and the wires on the poles by the sandy shoulders of the road swooped and dipped in the rhythm of an endless ballad. The bodies of the travellers glowed beneath the cotton dresses of the women and the cotton shirts of the men, and Sister Agnes's heavy features softened gradually and in them could be seen the outlines of the girl she had been in the meadow grasses and on the hard ridges of the farm in Kvinnesdalen.

# 6

The caravan of friends, with Florence Hagen's father's Packard in the lead, turns off the road from Green Lane into the camp grounds, down the entrance lane bordered with arbor vitae, and sweeps past the great tabernacle. Then around a bend, on the left the little tabernacle, nearly hidden in a grove of trees, on the right a field with long lines of painted cabins. Then another grove in which tents are pitched. When the camp meetings start in another month the grove will be full of people, with scarcely room for another tent, long lines for the washing up and the shower huts and the laundry tubs, noisy children in striped polo shirts running everywhere.

Two workmen paint a stack of iron bedsteads with sticky brown paint, and stuff striped ticking with straw from a yellow dusty heap for the people who will pay fifty cents a day to the camp manager Brother Lazarus for the little cabins, each with one window and one door, no plumbing and one light bulb, baking hot in the day but dry and sweet-smelling at night when people return from the great tabernacle, souls on fire and lips burbling still the ineffable language of heaven.

Further along, the little convoy passes the communal dining hall and dormitory for the winter Bible students, with its cupola on top and scullery shed at the back and wisps of smoke rising from a blackened midden among the trees. Then the lane becomes a grassy track, sloping downward through open woods, ash and poplar above, dogwood and root beer-smelling sassafras below, ending at last in a small clearing, where the cars stop. From here the company get out and walk down a well-beaten path with hand railings in the roughest spots and split logs for steps, and switchbacks to make the decline easier.

The picnic baskets and jugs and bottles, the canvas chairs and guitars, the blankets and changes of clothes, distribute themselves among the company, who troop in single file carrying their various burdens lightly and carelessly with many whoops of anticipated pleasure, and shouts from Brother Bringsrud about a loose log, a patch of mud, snakes, poison ivy. All his earnest warnings greeted with fresh outbreaks of mock terror and hilarity from the factory girls and the typists. Brother Bringsrud doesn't mind. He frequently takes off his hat, wipes his brow, and puts his hat back on.

Ole Knudsen in the lead, pretends to fall, or to drop something, and grins broadly. Florence Hagen sticks out her tongue and tosses her hair. Ragnar Sivertsen stations himself in the difficult places and with his free hand helps the factory girls and typists and Sister Agnes and Sister Sara, who has a large straw hat on and smiles coquettishly at Ragnar, to his deep embarrassment. Sister Patsy trails behind everyone, carrying nothing, sniffing finely the fugitive essences from the woods around, a faint smile on her lips, her eyes far away.

Perkiomen Creek winds along a deep valley floor with springy green banks and smooth rock ledges, sometimes deep and quiet with clear pools among the rocks, other times rapid and tumbling, where the rock ledges lie along its path. Dragonflies hover here and there on their business. Little else moves in the hot sun.

The company settles itself on a grassy patch at the upper end of a large rock with an easy slope into the water. Just in front of the rock the creek forms gentle rapids, but on the downstream side, to the left, is a partly-shaded pool with a sandy bottom, judged to be perfect for the baptism.

The factory girls and the typists take off their shoes and socks, and stand in the little rapids where they go over the foot of the rock. Then they dash back, leaving wet footprints on the rock. Ragnar sees to setting up the folding chairs for Brother Bringsrud and Sister Patsy and the Norwegian sisters. Sister Agnes spreads blankets on the ground, while Sister Sara sets out the fish pudding. Neen and Florence Hagen open hampers and put the jars of cold drinks in the shade, and fill with lemonade the cheerful painted glasses Florence brought to drink from.

Soon they are eating sandwiches and potato salad from Florence's hampers and having a taste of the fish pudding, which turns out to be a hit with everyone.

"That's not fish. It don't taste so bad," says one of the typists.

"You should eat more fish," Sister Sara replies sententiously from under her hat. "At home we had fish nearly every day. Fish and potatoes."

"I can't go near the fish store, it smells so bad," the typist says.

Ole Knudsen holds his nose. "Something is pretty fishy around here," he says, and backs away in mock horror, towards the water.

Two of the typists jump up and rush him. He waves his arms as though losing his balance. When they try to push him in he grabs them by their wrists and pulls them off balance so they stumble helplessly into the water up to their knees. Laughing, they splash him where he stands on the rock, grinning, arms akimbo, and get water on Sister Agnes and Brother Bringsrud, who also laugh. They all laugh, and settle down to eating.

When they have finished, and collect the scraps and wrap up the leftovers, the sun is directly overhead, and Sister Patsy decides it is time for Neen's baptism.

# 7

There was good times on Franklin Street. Pop worked for Landis, out at the end of Potomac Street, where they made machine tools. They had nice things, and the girls went to First Brethren and kept their prayer caps on the shelves in the vestibule, because at First Brethren they didn't wear them all the time the way the girls in the country did, but only in church. Ma was happy on Franklin Street. There was a little railroad still ran up to Mont Alto in the summer, and a place you could get ice cream and watch people dance in the big pavilion by the old iron works that Ma's dad had worked at all his life.

There's only two kids is younger than Neen, but six at home still, and Pop walked out on his job at Landis because nobody could tell him what to do. No, not him, even though jobs was already hard to find. They moved back to Wayne Hill, and Ma cried about it. Later it was Wayne Heights and real nice, but in those days Wayne Hill was just a mud street, and a long walk to school, which is up on the Five Forks road, past the houses of the Landis workers and the shoe-factory workers. The kids on the way to school call Neen nigger because she is dark-skinned and has bare feet and she has to come down past Razor Alley. They hadn't yet burned out the niggers in Razor Alley.

Pop was a slender man, with white skin and wavy black hair. He had a small heart-shaped face and bushy eyebrows always raised in a curve, especially one of them, so there was permanent lines over that eye. He had a bad temper. He threatened to kill all the children and himself that night on Franklin Street when they were evicted. Ma said you've got these kids to support. There's six still at home. And by God you're going to be a man and support them and you're not going to kill yourself or anybody else.

He didn't kill himself, and after a while got a team of horses which he took good care of, washing and combing them, and seeing they had the best oats, and went around to the farms and the orchards and hired himself and his team out by the day.

Neen is eleven. Neen is home supposed to be watching Junior. Junior is in the street playing in the dirt and eating some of it, the way he always does. Ma is out cleaning for the Sprintzes that own the shoe factory. Neen likes to climb on a chair and look out the small high window by the stove at the back of the kitchen, which is a kind of shed on stilts at the back of the house, where Wayne Hill slopes over toward Cottage Street. She puts her arms on the sill and rests her chin on her arms and looks out over the back gardens of the factory workers' houses lower down the hill. Which she does this particular day and the first thing she sees is a boy, just below. He is little, like Junior, and he has nothing on but a shirt and he is peeing, right out in the open, facing her, and making his pee arc high up in the air before it splatters in the dirt, and it's like he's writing with it. Neen is eleven and begins to giggle.

She doesn't realize Pop is home. He hears the giggle and comes up quietly behind her before she knows he is there and looks out to see what it is she is looking at. He snatches her away from the window by her arm and kicks the chair away at the same time, scaring her and hurting her but she doesn't dare scream or say anything. He doesn't beat her. He just shakes her, and says she is filthy, anybody looking at that on purpose has a filthy mind, and he will always be watching her and will never trust her.

Neen learned that day that you can't protect yourself if somebody needs to hurt you. She learned that her capacity to absorb cruelty was nearly infinite. And, anyway, it always stopped after a while. People got tired even of cruelty.

When Neen was sixteen she went to a revival at the Calvary Assemblies of God Pentecostal Church on South Potomac Street opposite the fire hall and gave her heart to God. The evangelist was a man named Nimrod Parks who could see into people's minds by the aid of the Holy Ghost. He would say that there was someone there that night that had a guilty secret that God was dealing with them about and they were resisting, but nothing could be hid from God and soon could not be hid from anyone, and would that person stand, right now, have the courage to stand right up. That was all they had to do. And Nimrod Parks was always right. Night after night, he knew there was someone, and had them dead to rights, and that if they stood up their burden would be lifted from them. It always happened that if they was unsaved they would have a glorious salvation, with weeping and repentance and then with great joy, and sometimes be filled with the Holy Ghost, speaking in other tongues and falling to the ground, slain in the Spirit. And if they was saved already, they would break through to higher ground in the Lord, and ask forgiveness of this one and that one toward whom they had been cold or backbiting or had a harsh spirit, and would meet that person half way across the front of the church, and throw their arms around them and forgive them for whatever it was. At such times the entire congregation would be bathed in the love of God.

On the night that Neen was saved Nimrod Parks had preached a searching sermon on First Samuel Chapter Three and the calling of the prophet Samuel when he was a child and a servant in the house of the priest Eli. How the Lord had called in the night Samuel, Samuel. And Samuel thought it was Eli, and three times went to Eli, and three times Eli sent him to lie down again, except on the third time he told Samuel what to say, because Eli knew it was the Lord. And so when the Lord said Samuel, Samuel, for the fourth time, Samuel said Speak, for thy servant heareth. Then Samuel had to tell Eli what the Lord said to him, which was that the house of Eli was doomed, for the iniquity of his sons, because his sons had made themselves vile, and he hadn't restrained them.

Nimrod Parks acted all of this out, under the inspiration of the Holy Ghost, so that you saw the boy as if he was there in front of you in his apparent insignificance and lack of experience, and the old priest on his couch, near blind and ready to die, who you would think would be spared the bitter prophecy about his family and his seed, but was not to be spared.

Nimrod Parks made the gooseflesh stand out on your arms, when he called Samuel, Samuel the four times, turning his head to the side, so that it came not from him but from the four corners of the room, Samuel, Samuel.

Neen took the message of Nimrod Parks as addressed to her. For was she not young? And she was not just anybody, but served in the temple. For so she understood the fact that at First Brethren she kept her prayer cap on a shelf in the vestibule. And had she not many times thought there was a voice, or at least an urging in her, for something special? Had she not held herself back until now, and not answered directly with all her heart?

She did so now. With great convulsive sobs she said, Speak, for thy servant heareth.

Neen told her Ma that night, and the next morning told Pop when he came back for his breakfast in the middle of the morning. They agreed to come to hear Nimrod Parks that night together, the three of them. And Nimrod Parks looked directly at them and preached about the danger of hardening the heart and how the Lord could take a violent and rash temper and soften it in the fire of his love. When Nimrod Parks said there was one in the congregation with whom the Holy Ghost was struggling mightily, who was resisting because of a stiff-necked nature that should be surrendered on the altar of sacrifice that very night, Pop stood to his feet and went down to the front of the church and fell to his knees, and Ma and Neen with him and rejoiced that now everything was going to be all right, and they went home to bed with praises on their lips.

But the next evening Pop began drinking elderberry wine, which he made himself every year, and as he did his old nature returned and he told Ma and Neen that he would not go back, because Neen had told that man all about him, and he knew her for a sly one but had never thought it would come to this.

Ma went with Neen that night again and got saved herself, but it wasn't anything because Ma wasn't a sinner you could rejoice over saving, and she was too worn out to do anything more than she was doing already. The disappointment over Pop took the last hope out of her, and she had no more salvation than could just about take his sarcasm after this. The sisters in the church didn't take Ma up because what do you do with one more worn out woman with iron-grey hair tied in a bun and a shapeless dress whose husband has to be prayed for that doesn't come to church. There was a feeling they'd been used in some way, getting all excited about Pop and then being let down, and their resentment and embarrassment had no other focus but Ma, who'd let herself look older than Pop and hadn't encouraged him.

Soon Ma quit going to church.

In proportion as the sisters dropped Ma, they took up Neen, because they felt sorry for her, because she was dark-skinned and not pretty and lived on Wayne Hill. Even though she was only sixteen Neen was admitted to the inner circle of the church and sat in the choicest position in the congregation, which was about five rows back in the centre pews and just a little to the side, and took to wearing a small hat.

Neen attracted no boyfriends, and she couldn't play the piano and was too shy to speak. And so she was bound to have a call as a missionary the sisters felt. And Neen felt this too, and never forgot Nimrod Parks's sermon on the calling of Samuel, and frequently prayed Samuel's prayer, Speak, for thy servant heareth.

Neen received no call to the mission field, although she acquired for a time the gift of tongues. From the moment she received the Baptism in the Holy Ghost, which was the last night of Nimrod Parks, she had an unusual facility in tongues, which some said must be a real language, just like in the Book of Acts Chapter Two, and if Neen could find out what that was she would know where the call to be a missionary was. However that might be, there was no denying the authority of Neen's utterance, when she stood slowly in her seat, always at a tactful moment in the service, after the prayers, or just before the preacher got under way, or after a particularly powerful special number from the Ladies' Trio, who always wore white blouses and little red bows at the neck when they were going to sing, or from Brother Ethan Calimer, who sang tenor solos. Then Neen would begin in a clear voice straight away, and not the usual blubbering, so you could hear every word distinctly, although you didn't know the words of course.

Usually there was an interpretation, from Sister Wenger as often as not, the pastor's wife, but these were unsatisfactory, and many thought were of the flesh rather than of the Holy Ghost, and were certainly no reply to Neen's unspoken ache on these occasions. Speak, for thy servant heareth.

And then this gift faded, and Neen stopped sitting in the special place that was just behind the children on the fifth row, but moved in among the married people further back and made herself small.

She got work at the J.C.Penney on Main Street showing gloves and stockings to the wives and daughters of the town's mill owners and lawyers and doctors, and lived at home and helped Ma, who was not very strong, although she was a big woman still, and no one realized she had not long to live.

Gradually, Neen came to feel that her calling had been a delusion. Worse, that Pop was right after all. There was a corrupt seed in her, a germ of filthiness. Her salvation had been like the white prayer caps on the shelf in the vestibule at First Brethren, something put on for church, but no better than filthy rags in the sight of the all-seeing God. And the rest of Nimrod Parks's sermon came back to her, and she returned again and again to First Samuel Chapters Three and Four. She was not like Samuel but more like the vile sons of the priest Eli, for whom even the precious Ark of the Covenant was no protection, and it was her fault Pop was not saved and never would be and Ma had her hopes dashed.

The summer Neen was nineteen Ma died of a cancer and Sister Patsy came to Calvary Assemblies of God.

Sister Patsy took her out of herself. Neen crept down to the second row, a row at a time, over the course of the special meetings, just to see her better. She gazed on Sister Patsy's ankle, which was covered in white lisle of the faintest iridescent shimmer that Neen knew you could not buy at the J.C.Penney, and the bone was light and squarish and the bit of calf visible below the modest hem of her dress was underdeveloped, like a girl, and made a funny ache in Neen's chest under her arm and in her throat. For Sister Patsy did not stand behind the pulpit like Pastor Wenger. Nor like Nimrod Parks, with his great weather-beaten face, standing in it, and above it, clutching it on both sides in his great fists like Jehu in his chariot. No, Sister Patsy was everything in her own body and needed nothing and was just herself, and all the space around her was the same. She stood sideways sometimes and preached just to Lila Drumheller that played the piano and sat over against the wall, next to the piano in case she was needed for the altar call. How Neen envied Lila Drumheller, who had hair on her face and a squint, and was nearly beautiful the way she looked when Sister Patsy preached to her that way.

Sister Patsy had a way of using words that you used all the time, and never really thought about what they meant, and she would repeat them over and over, and make the congregation say them after her. Like Sin, which she said slowly and with a hissing sound. S-s-s-s-i-n-n. Like that. Or she would say Jesus in the softest way, J-e-e-z-z-z-u-z-z. Like that. And she said the thing was in the sound of it, and you could get inside it by the way you said it. And it was like the part of you that was God would be stirred into life, and blossom like the flowers of the field.

And Neen repeated these words after Sister Patsy until they lost their sense and the power that they had over her that came from outside of her. The sin that punished you, Sister Patsy seemed to say, was only a word, and the power of it lay in the word. By uttering it over and over without fear, making the dreadful hiss in it ridiculous, you got power over it. Sister Patsy got you to laugh at the silliness of it. When Neen said the name of Jesus, tasting the beautiful sound for its own sake, then Jesus was not outside of her looking sorrowfully at her, but someone who was inside of her that she could love, and who loved her.

On the last night of the special meetings, Neen asked Sister Patsy if she could come with her and help her in her ministry, for she had a gift of the Holy Ghost, and had waited for a call, but none came, and now her Ma was dead. Sister Patsy said she was going to New York City to answer the call of a church there. If Neen wasn't afraid she could come along.

This was at the front of the church after everyone had gone, except there were still some voices from out by the door saying good night, but hushed, because the service had been hushed and beautiful, and people had been lifted out of themselves for a little while, and had seen inside themselves and seen the character of Christ there. Tomorrow they would forget it and feel foolish, but tonight they were so many gods picking their way homeward.

Sister Patsy was sitting on the edge of the platform. Her violet eyes were dark and the skin around them was dark. She said that if Neen wasn't afraid she could come along, and Neen collapsed on the floor at her feet and cried for joy.

# 8

Sister Patsy and Neen change in the woods into white robes. When they appear again Sister Patsy wades into the water in a little patch of sunlight over the pool. Her fair hair shines in the sun.

The little company stand on the rock looking down. Neen waits on the edge of the pool, as Sister Patsy speaks.

"Our dear Sister Neen has decided to follow the Lord in Baptism. Come to me, Sister Neen."

Neen is already walking into the water, and when she comes to Sister Patsy, Sister Patsy turns and walks beside her into the deepest part of the pool, until the water is at their waists and their gowns float out from them a bit and they pause to push them down until the skirts are weighted with water.

Then Sister Patsy raises her arms and speaks slowly, as though to children.

"The river runs where it wishes, through all the work of God and through all the works of man.

"This rock cannot stop the river, nor can the great city. The river keeps in its channel for a little while, and then it escapes.

"When we step into this river we share in this escape. We are the quicksilver light of the surface, and the gold that dapples the sand below, that no man can say here it is, or there, or I am sure of it."

Then in one motion Sister Patsy takes Neen between her hands, by the back and chest, and plunges her backwards under the water. Sister Patsy stumbles and disappears herself for a moment, but brings them both again to the surface, faces uplifted and hair streaming. They walk together toward the shore, Sister Patsy holding Neen's hand, Sister Agnes remembering just in time to meet them with two large towels, which they put around themselves and walk slowly back to the woods to change again into their clothes.

As a result of the Baptism the electricity between Ole Knudsen and Florence Hagen becomes a deeper pressure, expressed in the strong curve of her back, and a tautness in her hips, in the tension in Ole's jaw and in the way he shades his eyes with one hand and thrusts the other in his pocket. For the rest of the day they avoid their usual banter, and scarcely talk to one another, but their bodies strike poses that are for one another, and their movements are unnecessarily graceful over the most ordinary tasks.

Ragnar Sivertsen breaks away from the group and finds a place upstream by a shallow stretch of the creek, where he skips stones furiously.

The two Norwegian Sisters dab their eyes and make little noises to one another in Norwegian, before settling down in the canvas chairs.

Brother Bringsrud thinks to himself that there is something strange about what he has just seen, and that he must think about it some more. It occurs to him that there were no words about The Father, The Son and The Holy Ghost, which are always said by the Friends. He is sure it is in the Bible, but for now he cannot think of where that is. He will look it up another time.

It is not in Brother Bringsrud's nature to be a legalist, which is something anyway the gospel has freed Christians from, unlike the Jews. But Brother Bringsrud also knows that the devil enters by small compromises with gospel order. He is the eldest here, and also a man and therefore not given to weakness as are the women, even if they are called of the Lord because so few men answer the call in these latter days. Not for the first time, Brother Bringsrud wonders if baptizing people in the tank under the floor were not the safest thing after all.

The day passes quietly. The young people go exploring, and return with bits of driftwood and coloured stones. Sister Agnes takes out some knitting, and Brother Bringsrud sleeps on the rock with his hat over his face. Sister Sara reads a book.

Late in the afternoon, when the light has softened, Ragnar and Ole make a small fire, under Brother Bringsrud's expert direction. Sister Sara produces a coffee pot and fills it with water from the creek. When the water is boiling on the little fire, she stirs in a handful of coarsely ground coffee, the strongest blend from the A&P, and a pinch of salt, moves the pot off the centre of the fire to steep, and fetches the buttered waffles and the sugared wild cranberries, which have been saved for this moment.

Guitars are brought out and all join in singing old camp-meeting and gospel songs. Florence Hagen has a strong clear voice and leads them through the third and fourth stanzas that the others don't know so well. Sister Agnes and Sister Sara agree to sing in Norwegian. Their last number "Day by Day," which they sing in both Norwegian and English, brings tears to everyone's eyes, especially the line, "He who has for me a father's heart."

They all sit for a long time, looking into the fire.

Sister Patsy breaks the silence, "Brother Bringsrud, you must know some edifying tales of the old times in Norway. You must tell us a story."

At this the factory girls and typists chorus Yes and Oh, do, and pull their cheap sweaters tighter around their shoulders. Ragnar looks up with keen interest, and Ole inches closer to Florence. Brother Bringsrud clears his throat and tells the following story.

# 9

"This is a story my mother told," Brother Bringsrud began, "from the time when she was a young girl in a poor mountain district in Norway.

"In those days each parish had only one schoolmaster, who had different circuits on different days of the week. The children gathered at one of the farms when it was their day for him to come, and the schoolmaster taught them their letters, and to add and subtract, and Norwegian history, when the weather was good and the children weren't needed with the hay.

"At fourteen, the children learned the Our Father and the Ten Commandments from the priest. Then the bishop on his next visit examined them, and if they could recite the Our Father and the Ten Commandments without mistakes they were confirmed, and from that time they were grown up and had to look out for themselves, and stay clear of the devil and the bailiff as best they could.

"Grandfather was the schoolmaster in the parish, and also a follower of Hans Nilsen Hauge, who was a preacher of the gospel and tried to better conditions for the small farmers.

Hauge showed them how to be independent, and start small industries, and not waste themselves in drunkenness. For this they persecuted him, the priests and the officials, and put him in prison and broke his spirit. But the memory of him stayed alive and is alive to this day.

"And so Grandfather spoke to the people at the farms, wherever he taught the children, about the foolishness of drinking, and of dancing to the fiddle, especially at weddings and funerals. For people got drunk and did wicked things, and wasted their money and their goods. Many people lost their farms and had to leave the country because of it, and children went hungry.

"The priest didn't like Grandfather interfering with the people. He told Grandfather—in his fancy way, just like Danish, with marbles in his mouth—that those were good old Norwegian ways, the fiddle playing and the drinking. Didn't he know that people came from the university to write down the songs and make notes on the dances, and learn the words that people used for things. Grandfather was not in the spirit of the times. Modern Christians didn't accuse people by talking about hell and sin and the devil all the time.

"This priest had two sons, who were famous in the districts all around for their devilment, which the priest turned a blind eye to, being widowed, and a man of learning who got letters and parcels from as far away as Lund—or so the postmistress said.

"These wicked sons never tired of tormenting Grandfather. When they saw his horse tied somewhere they set it free to wander in the woods. They sank the little boat he used for rowing over the lake on one of his circuits. They teased my mother when she was alone with the goats up on the mountain, hoping to stir Grandfather up and make him lose his temper, so they could say he wasn't the fine Christian he set himself up for.

"To add to Grandfather's troubles, Grandmother worried constantly, and was not always well, and missed the farm she had come from as a girl, and thought that Grandfather had brought these troubles on himself by disturbing folks with things that were none of his business.

"One day, Grandfather was riding his horse alone through a narrow valley as the sun was about to set, not far from his poor farm, thinking on the persecutions of the priest's two evil sons, and praying to the Lord for strength, when he met the devil for the first time. The devil was standing in his path, next to a little stone bridge, a thing of cunning work that folk said was made by the netherworld people in olden times.

"Now this valley was well known in those parts, for old people said they had heard the netherworld folk driving their flocks through this valley and calling to one another, and they said it was best when you heard them to turn and go another way. They said, however, that a certain poor man in the time of the priest Schilderup (this was in the old Catholic time) stole a cow from the underworld people by throwing his knife over it, which broke the charm on it, and that man became rich afterwards. For they say that steel thrown over any enchanted thing will break the spell, and whoever succeeds in doing this is the owner of the thing from that time forward.

"Anyway, there the devil stood, blocking Grandfather's way. Grandfather said the devil was dressed in an old-fashioned suit of white wool, the trousers wide at the bottom, with buttons, and leather in the seat, a short jacket that opened out in the front to show the red lining, with a double row of buttons, and also buttons at the cuffs. He had on a fine broad-brimmed hat and shiny boots. He was not young and not old, and foreign in his features. Not like a Finn. Perhaps like a Jew. Not very tall, but broad and vigorous.

"As Grandfather approached, the devil made no sign, but waited until Grandfather came abreast. Grandfather reined in his horse. The devil said to him, 'Are you here too?'

"Just like that, 'Are you here too?'

"Now this was something uncles liked to say when they saw you somewhere. At church, you know, or at a bailiff's auction, as though they had surprised themselves by being there at all, and, of all things, seeing someone they knew. Of course this was a joke, because they always knew everybody there. They said 'Are you here too?' to test the wits of the young fellows, who stare with their jaws open until they see that they are being made fun of, and learn to give the right answer, which is 'Oh, yes. I am here. Are you here too?' Then the uncle winks, and maybe puts a coin in your breast pocket, and goes to look for someone else.

"That was just the way the devil said it, 'Are you here too?', and in a rich voice, and good Norwegian, not like the priest's but like the king's officials who come from Christiania, a singing sound, deep and high at the same time, that has the world beyond the mountains in it.

"Grandfather, quick as a flash, for he had a good wit, and was not afraid in the least, for he had his Bible in a skin case tied on behind him, said 'No, I am not here. I am home having salt mutton and cabbage and flatbread with my wife and baby.'

"Grandfather then spurred his horse to a quick walk and didn't look back until he arrived home safely.

"In the weeks that followed, the two wicked sons of the priest increased their persecution. They took down the stones of the pen where Grandfather kept his sheep, which meant he spent a whole day on the mountain to find them again. Then they moved the markers in the woods that showed where Grandfather's rights to gather wood ended, and made it look as though he had been trying to cheat his neighbour, whose farm was in the next parish, and who was famous for his bad temper and iron fists. Fortunately, while out in the woods collecting bundles of sticks for the fire, Grandfather saw that the stone markers had been moved, and set them right. He said nothing to anyone, and kept his counsel, because he could see it was the devil's work.

"Some time after this he was rowing across the lake, on his most difficult circuit. There was a thick fog on the lake, so that he could not see the other side. As he passed a little island that told him he was on the right course, he saw the devil, dressed as before, sitting on a rock on the island, right on the water's edge.

"Again the devil said, as Grandfather pulled even with him, 'Are you here too?'

"Grandfather thought perhaps this time the devil looked a little thinner. His clothes were not so fresh, and his face was haggard.

"Grandfather looked directly in the devil's eyes and said in a level voice, 'Naturally, I am here too. But I can't stay to talk. I am a busy man, and the children are waiting.'

"He continued rowing, and watched the devil until the fog hid him from view, and soon got to the other shore.

"After that, things went even worse for Grandfather. Not only did the priest's sons think of new and more aggravating tricks to play, but the whole parish seemed in a bad spirit. The children would not listen when he taught them. The young ones were sickly and snivelled over their lessons. The older ones fought and were insolent, even those that were usually good and could normally be counted on to help the younger ones.

"On top of this there were two deaths in the district, one right after the other, and folk said there was something suspicious about it. No one could remember two funerals at Whitsuntide before.

"One of the dead men was an old bachelor who was rotting in the woods already when they found him. The other was Berto Tveit, who in those days was the biggest man in the district and had twenty cows and four horses. There was no sign of illness beforehand, and he had just married Maren Gundersdatter, the widow of Sergeant Kristjer Aslaksen who had been to Copenhagen as a young man and had once been a member of the legislature representing the farmers. Maren Gundersdatter was, in short, a widow twice in the space of a year, and now very rich. But Maren Gundersdatter was not much liked in the district. There were whispers that she had a baby when she was young and hid it, and it died, or the netherworld people came for it.

"Nevertheless, when the word went around that Maren Gundersdatter was going to give her husband the biggest funeral ever seen in that part of the world, and had hired the most famous fiddlers in Norway, and was paying specie dollars for the best ale and cakes, people forgot that she was not a good woman. They prepared their finery, and dusted off all the old feuds with their neighbours, and put new hope into plans to marry off their sons and daughters, even the ugly ones, because at a funeral like this surprising things happen under cover of drink and the night and even in broad daylight. Many boasted of soon settling scores. Others began to dream of the advantages to themselves of rich in-laws.

"Grandfather was in despair. He saw all the work of the Lord being undone and set back for many years. He gave himself to days of fasting and prayer, and could be heard groaning to himself in heaviness of spirit as he rode about his circuits.

"The eve of Berto Tveit's funeral was cold and crisp. A silvery moon shone over the tops of the mountains on the edge of the parish, and over the water of great Otra, the river that comes from the high glaciers and flows all the way to Kristiansand in the Southland.

"On this very night Grandfather was returning home from the prayer house, which sat on a bit of rocky ground near the nickel mines in the centre of the parish. The heavens were made of brass, as they used to say, meaning that the prayers of the little group that had been gathered at the prayer house seemed to go nowhere but up to the ceiling.

"Grandfather was on foot, as his horse was lame. He had not gone very far when he saw the devil for the third time.

"The devil sat on a heap of broken rock from an abandoned digging, where people sometimes went hunting for pretty bits of stone that they polished into jewellery. Grandfather could see, even by the moonlight, that the devil was not well. His shoes were scuffed and dirty. His trouser bottoms were fouled and there were buttons hanging by a thread and one was missing. He wore an old shawl that didn't quite cover what had once been his fine white jacket. The lining had sagged below the skirt, and Grandfather could see a rip under the arm. The devil had no hat on at all, and his hair was uncombed. He was wiping snot on his sleeve with an absent air when he noticed Grandfather.

"'Are you here too?' the devil sighed, as though this were a matter of indifference, playing this game with Grandfather. He seemed mad, and yet also like an old actor playing mad. Grandfather thought it best not to say anything.

"'See here, Skjeggestad,' the devil said abruptly, using the name of the farm Grandfather owned, and which his ancestors had owned before him. 'See here Skjeggestad, I will come clean with you.'

"The devil pulled himself upright and fished for something in his pocket.

"'You think you are brave and clever opposing me, don't you?'

"Grandfather said nothing.

"The devil shrugged. 'You wouldn't get very far if I were myself.'

"'The truth is, Skjeggestad, I rather like you,' the devil continued after a pause, 'and I am tired of this blasted country.' (The devil used rougher language than this, which I cannot repeat in front of young people.)

"'It is too much work here for small potatoes, silly tricks that aren't any fun anymore. I need a change of air. I am thinking of moving to America. All the best people have gone there. I could live easy, and have more help. You see what this place does to me.'

"The devil gestured to his clothes.

"'I have passage booked for tomorrow, Skjeggestad. But there are loose ends.'

"The devil gave a long speculative look at Grandfather, who still remained silent.

"'Ah, yes— Well, I will come to the point.'

"The devil paused. 'In short, Skjeggestad, I am surrendering the field to you.'

"At this, the devil opened his palm, there in the moonlight, and put in Grandfather's hand a small knife in a plain leather sheath.

"Grandfather pulled the knife out of its sheath. It was the most beautiful thing he had ever seen. The handle was made of dark silky wood and carved in the shape of a woman. Her hair swirled down her naked back and around her hips to her small round belly. Her arms were held close to her body, a hand covering each breast. The tiny fingernails of the hands were utterly lifelike, and shone in the silver light, against the dark wood, like miniature pearls. Grandfather held it in his hand to test the feel and the balance, first this way and then that way. It could have been made just for him alone.

"The blade made every other blade seem a clumsy thing good only for shaving kindling for the fire. It was thin and curved slightly back on itself, with a design engraved on it. When Grandfather tested it on his thumb it drew a fine line of blood.

"The devil could see that Grandfather coveted this knife in spite of himself. He leaned more closely and dropped his voice into a wheedling throb that made Grandfather's head swim.

"'Made for me, that was, in the last of the netherworld smithies, beneath Burning Peak. The smith himself took the steel from the mound above Senum, on the ridge overlooking Otra, from a blade forged in Novgorod and buried at Senum with a great chief renowned for slaughter in the old Viking time.

"'I brought him the handle myself. The wood is of the tree on which Iscariot hanged himself, from a piece in the secret collection of the Black Elector, carved for me in the far south by the Master of the Virgin in Majesty.

"'The hands? Nails to the life, are they not?'

"The devil chuckled, and waited as Grandfather stared at the unearthly woman. The devil's voice fell to a whisper.

"'Real nails, those are. Torn from babies born to desperate maids, alone, in the summer on the high heath, and drowned, unbaptised, in pools in the peat. Only the little finger of the left hand. It took me many centuries to collect that set. A foolish indulgence, but worth the trouble. Don't you think, Skjeggestad?'

"Grandfather wanted to fling the obscene thing from him, but he found himself powerless to do anything. The devil saw that he had an advantage and pressed on, leaning even closer, speaking directly into Grandfather's ear.

"'Tomorrow, at the funeral feast for Tveit, I will give you an opportunity you have only dreamed of. You will have no more opposition after tomorrow. Everything will go your way from now on. Remember only this,

*Life you shall command,*
*When steel flies in air—*'

"It was as though there were more lines, but they never came. Without finishing, the devil disappeared. Not all at once with a bang. Not even slowly fading. It was as when a pattern of light and shade, without moving, becomes a different shape in the mind. A vase becomes two faces, or a cloud becomes first a snail, and then a lady in a hat. Where Grandfather had seen the devil only a moment before there were now only the rocks in the moonlight. He stepped back, and squinted, and then came forward again and reached out carefully toward the rocks. Nothing. He looked down at the knife, real enough there in his hand. He put it carefully in its sheath, which he threaded onto his belt by the leather loop, and walked home deep in thought.

"In the morning Grandfather had his boiled egg and crispbread with honey, and silently made his preparations for the day. He put on his best breeches and waistcoat, both of which had been black once, but were now green from age and wear, and wrapped his lower legs against the cold. Lastly, he put on his greatcoat and tied a scarf around his neck, and put his Bible in a knapsack with a turnip and a piece of rye bread for his lunch. Grandmother had never seen him so full of grim purpose, and neglected to nag him about fixing the draught on the stove. Mother remembers that day perfectly well, because Grandfather whistled in the house, and put his shoes on the table while oiling them, which Grandmother never permitted, having been raised to believe that these things called the devil.

"About the rest of that day, and what happened at Berto Tveit's funeral, Grandfather never said much, but the whole district was there and many stories were told about it. If you leave out the exaggerations, this is what seems to have taken place.

"There was never before seen so much food as Maren Gundersdatter had put out on trestles in the yard at Tveit. Not to mention many great barrels of ale and many small ones of strong spirits. A space of beaten earth was prepared for the dancing. The fiddle players took turns on a raised platform in the centre, and sometimes played contests with each other.

"Folk got red in the face from the food and the drink. The pretty dances of the maidens gave way to the young men showing their bold steps and high jumps, with a flash of the silver-mounted knives in their belts and their broad leathern bottoms creaking, that made a twist in the guts of the maidens and a flush in their cheeks. From time to time a bold lad would pluck a stout matron from the crowd and whirl her off her feet until her breath went right away and she would sit down abruptly, and not always very modestly. The jokes became less and less such as decent folk should hear.

"Grandfather could be seen here and there as the day wore on in this way, talking pleasantly with the more sober farmers, and patting the heads of his charges.

"Already some fights had begun, and then broken off, with muttered swearing to have another go at so-and-so later, who was no better than a pig's snout, or other words that were worse than that. Still Grandfather kept apart, with a tight smile on his lips. He ate his own poor lunch alone, and waited.

"Then it happened, that everyone remembered for years afterwards. There was a sound of hallooing from the direction of the river, and some runners came, all out of breath so you couldn't tell what they were saying. The fiddling came to a halt and a hush settled over the great yard. From the near corner of the wood before Tveit a shuffling body of men and boys appeared carrying a litter of birch poles and sailcloth with something dark and wet on it that soon resolved itself into the body of a young man still in his boots, and weeds on his legs and his coat.

"Before it could be seen who it was on the dreadful bier—there was no doubt it was a dead man approaching—people's eyes darted here and there counting their loved ones, seeing who was missing in their own households and from among their neighbours.

"Whispers passed from the back to the front of the crowd, and washed over the trestle tables and on to the porch and up to the farmhouse itself, where the poor widows of the parish still came and went through the entrance hall, in ignorance of events, carrying in their hands the best pewter beakers and trenchers from Maren Gundersdatter's dressers, waiting on the priest, the local representative to the legislature, the sheriff and two professors from the university, all of whom sat within by the fire smoking pipes.

"The whispers at last penetrated this sanctuary in the person of the sexton, with his hat in his hand like a figure in a painting, as the corpse on its sailcloth bed approached the steps and was laid on the edge of the porch.

"All eyes were now on the darkened doorway, from which presently emerged the priest, blinking in the light and pulling his coat around his shoulders. He had the air of one who perhaps thought the dignity of his office and his modern, liberal views ought to have earned him some exemption from sorrow.

"But he discovered he was only a man, and sank to his knees before the body of his eldest son.

"For that was who the drowned man was, without any doubt,

the firstborn of the priest's two evil sons. He had been out on the river, on a dare, walking on the logs which were destined for the sawmills down the river and corralled in great jams near the shore at this time of year. Somehow the logs shifted. He slipped and fell between them. The logs closed over him, and he was drowned before his friends could move them.

"No one knew what to do, of course. Even the sheriff was stunned, when he came out, at the sight of the priest collapsed there and the dead boy, and the great hushed crowd. Everyone remembers that Grandfather was the first to move. Some say they saw him go deathly white when the whispers first reached him. Others say they saw no change in him until he came forward. All agree that he stepped on to the porch and stood at the foot of the dead man, and that he had a knife, a small fancy one, in his right hand, with the sheath in his left hand, and that a struggle seemed to be going on in his soul, and sweat stood out on his forehead in great drops.

"Either the sheriff approached him, or he looked around and saw the sheriff, but the presence of this official seemed to trigger a return to his senses, and Grandfather, without having said a word, left the porch, went out through the yard, and away in the direction of the river, where, some said later, they saw him throw the knife out into the water as far as he could throw it.

"The drowned boy was buried in the churchyard. The priest

caused to have written on his stone, after his name and the dates of his birth and death, the words Otra Took Him, and nothing more, where you can read it to this day. People knew the priest was not right in his mind, for it was not a Christian thing to put on a gravestone.

"Soon there was a new parish priest. Maren Gundersdatter married again. And folk found new things to talk about.

"Not long afterwards, Grandfather moved away from the district. He sold the farm where his ancestors had lived, and with the proceeds bought a small holding on the coast, near Grimstad, where he worked in a shipping office and sometimes wrote amusing articles in dialect for the newspapers.

"Eventually he told my mother what I have told you today about his meetings with the devil. He never preached again, but Mother said he often prayed alone, far into the night. He spoke often, with sorrow, of the sin of pride, and how the devil, who is a liar and the father of lies, destroys those who are lifted up in their own conceit."

act three

# 1

Sister Patsy entered Ebenezer by the front door, turning the key with effort and holding it down against the tumblers while she tugged at the heavy door with her free hand. Once inside, she shut and bolted the door, descended the short flight of steps and stepped into the church. Immediately, she knew someone was in the building with her.

She carefully shut the inner door behind her. She stood underneath the clock, her hands on the back of the last pew and looked out over the auditorium, at the rows of varnished pews, smelling of lemon oil, the piano on the platform, the curtain backdrop, and her own reading stand in the middle.

Sister Patsy never entered this place without anticipation. It was her practice always to come early, before anyone else had arrived, to take in the atmosphere, sniff the elements, the drift, the layered particles of spirit, like eddies of motes in the dusty air. She liked to watch the alterations of light as the high afternoon gave way to late afternoon and then to evening, even though the sun hardly shone directly into the auditorium, only a very little bit through the windows along the left side, where the building next door stopped and left a space for the setting sun. There was a moment when this bit of light turned the varnished pews the colour of old gold, and the empty space became a palpable thing, turbid with an inexpressible longing, for which the building and its furniture were only a shell and could scarcely contain it.

In these moments, alone in this expectancy, Sister Patsy received the things she would say in the meeting that followed. If it would be a comforting word, spun from the sounds of humming and whispering and a mother's soothing murmur. Or teasing and skipping, dancing on ahead like a child, beguiling and taunting, strewing apples, and circlets of saxifrage and scabious, sporting the bangles she received from her Lord in his hay-mow or on the prow of his bridal barge or on his couch of caressing and of laughter.

There were other days, when Sister Patsy received words of war and contradiction, sounds of hissing and the flapping of bat's wings, when she felt driven nearly mad, encircled with darkness and the sounds of wasps, when her mouth could not suppress these sounds but struggled through them until from afar came the clash of war mace on breastplate, the bright sound of steel and the neighing of horses.

Sister Patsy had never understood the necessity for separating people into the saved and the unsaved. It would have shocked most of the people who heard her if they could have known the extent of her indifference to what they thought of as the gospel. Her interest in people was in the quality of their souls. There were many dull and distracted souls. But there were also winged souls, souls with the sinews of an athlete, souls with purpose and hope, souls that were beautiful, that needed only the kiss of awakening to take flight, to live on the plane suitable to the human soul, which was Godlike. Like Jesus, arm and arm with his strong men, eating strong meat, drinking strong wine, confounding the Jews with his quiet voice, touching his friends, men and women, who sat at table with him.

There was little cure for defective and damaged souls in Sister Patsy's experience. She did not despise them. Nor did she pity them. She saw that the work to which she was called was the opening of the eyes of those who had God in them, who had Godlikeness as a seed in their nature, who were thus marked for a larger life in the light of beauty. She had no advice or method or system. Her gift was to sense the openings, to read correctly the state of the spiritual world and to incorporate this in her own peculiar aesthetic, in which sounds were smells, smells were colours, and sight was touch.

The exercise of this gift required real moments, real audiences, particular situations. It was a virtuoso performance on a difficult instrument. It could never be written down to be read. If it could, there would be nothing there, like musical notation to the tone deaf. Reduced to writing, Sister Patsy's finest moments she knew would be stripped bare, exposed as alliterative rubbish, the babblings of a deranged schoolgirl. The meeting was her medium. Her fame rested in the reports of great meetings. On the other hand, it made her vulnerable to exaggeration, to spiteful depreciation, to misrepresentation.

Sister Patsy never failed to move crowds of people, but afterwards, when people were alone with themselves, the dull felt cheated, sure they had been hoodwinked. They could not bear to think of themselves as dull, and thought instead how clever they were to see that it was a conjurer's trick after all, and regretted the fifty-cent piece dropped in the plate, and felt foolish, and then angry, and congratulated themselves at last with the thought that everything in the world is about money.

Those who were capable saw and felt what Sister Patsy saw and felt, and knew that it was outside of themselves and outside of Sister Patsy, and were changed, but each in his own way, in the unique way of the soul according to its planting and its nurturing and its seasons. And they were not of the crowd and kept what they knew in a secret part of themselves, because they could not explain it anyway, since that was not their gift.

So it was that Sister Patsy had used up her gift and her life. Those who were like her, and saw the things she saw, were quiet, and when she had passed they did not forget her but they did not speak of her either, or if they did it was only to one another in quiet recognition of a shared wonder. But the others piled up thickly around her, an accumulating tide of doubters, wondering, as they whispered to one another, if everything about Sister Patsy was quite of the Lord. The district superintendents, and the teachers in the Bible schools, and the pastors of the big churches, were not as keen to invite her to address their camp meetings and chapel meetings, and to take their pulpits for revival meetings, as they had been at the beginning.

For all Sister Patsy's apparent confidence, she was shaken by a resistance that was formless but growing, and that struck at the integrity of her gift, which she had never sought but which had found her—to the cost of Brother Clutterbuck, as she sometimes now reflected.

In this moment, in the stillness in Ebenezer, in the clear sense that someone or something was in the building with her, Sister Patsy faced fully for the first time that she had come here to this place because she had run out of charmed flight, run out of the will to ignore or to neutralize the resistance to her. She was a creature gone to ground, gone instinctively to this place she was meant to wait in, until the danger passed, or until she was changed, like a moth or butterfly, and flew away.

The fight in her was suspended, not least because she did not know what powers were on her side and what powers were ranged against her. The encounter with Nathalie Thornquist that morning disturbed her now as it had not at the time. She had had no illusions about the capacity of the Thornquist woman to cause trouble, but what she now realized in her heightened sensitivity, was the hatred of the woman for her, and the reason for it. It was not that Nathalie Thornquist could not grasp the things of the spirit, or that she had never been a soul touched by beauty. She had become blighted in some way. Deformed in soul and spirit. She had rejected beauty, and now hated it.

More disturbing yet, Sister Patsy sensed that Nathalie Thornquist had something powerful on her side. Although she was a preposterous woman, the preposterousness was mere detail, a cover for a distortion at the most fundamental level. Sister Patsy was not sure what this was. Was it the sort of evil she had faced in the playground at the Brethren camp many years ago? Perhaps it was not evil at all. Rather something akin to her own gift and opposed to it. Something from the grey cloud that followed her.

*Run, Patsy. Run*, it said.

It was saying it now. *Run, Patsy. Run.*

Sister Patsy felt alone and unprotected, as she had never felt before.

# 2

The sound of breaking crockery came from the kitchen. Then the voice of a man, a youth. Something coarse, muffled by the closed door between the kitchen and the auditorium.

Sister Patsy remained still and listened. She felt exhilaration, and relief. The mood of despair vanished.

A window opened. The crunch of broken glass stepped on. Scuffling. The window fell. Seconds later, fleeing shadows across the frosted panes of the windows on the right-hand side, meaning the intruder had come across behind the building and was now running along the narrow passage toward the street, where he had only to vault a low iron gate to make his escape.

All of Sister Patsy's senses were tuned, however, to something else. She moved silently to the kitchen, and opened the door, confirming only what she already surmised from the sounds. Someone had broken the window, opened the catch and climbed in, searched for something to steal, and on hearing Sister Patsy moving about the church, climbed out again, attempting at first to do it quietly, and then, having pushed a cup onto the tiled floor—the evidence lay in front of the sink—gave up all pretence of concealment, and scrabbled over the sill. So much was plain.

There was something else. Someone was still in the building.

Sister Patsy turned and thought for a moment, then moved swiftly across the front of the platform, down the farthest aisle to the rear of the auditorium, through the door of the cloakroom, and straight into the ladies' toilet.

The room was clean and sparsely furnished. The smells of disinfectant and floor drains mingled in the close atmosphere. Two stalls with varnished wooden doors that extended almost to the cement floor filled half of one wall. Opposite these, a wash basin with a small cloudy mirror above it, and next to that a length of rough cotton cloth sewn into a long loop and suspended from a wooden rod set high on the wall in wooden brackets. Then a wire waste basket with some crumpled paper in it, and a low cupboard for cleaning supplies. An old day-bed sat below a large frosted window that fronted on the street and provided the only source of light. The day-bed was covered with a yellow chenille spread. Mothers nursed their babies here before meeting, and sisters, overcome at lengthy tarrying services, composed themselves.

The cover was disturbed and on it were strewn articles of clothing, a striped polo shirt, a man's white shirt with the sleeves rolled up and the lower part creased as though it had been tied in a knot around someone's middle, and a pair of dirty green cotton slacks. On the floor in front of the day-bed were two very small, scuffed brown shoes.

Sister Patsy took this in at a glance. Without hesitating she pulled open the door of the nearest stall.

The creature in front of her was clearly very ill. A girl, naked except for striped socks with the toes out, sprawled on the brown wooden toilet seat, legs apart, leaning back against the upright lid, her arms slack at her side, her head lolling against the lead drain-pipe that ran from the water closet above.

She had been violently sick between her legs, spattering the bowl and herself. She was covered with a film of sweat and had removed her clothes in the delirium of fever and nausea.

Sister Patsy moved around beside the girl, and cradling her head in the crook of her right arm, reached across her and seized the end of the toilet paper roll and spun off a great length, wadding it up as best she could with one hand, and swabbed the worst from the girl's thighs. She reached between her legs and wiped her bottom. She dropped the wad in the bowl. Swiftly, automatically, ignoring the stench, she did this all a second time and pulled the chain.

The sound of the rushing water brought the girl around. Her head came forward and her eyes, which had been closed, focused briefly on Sister Patsy's. But Sister Patsy was already lifting her gently forward and onto her feet. Half carrying her, she brought the girl out to the basin and put the girl's hands on the wall so that she could support herself. She turned on the tap. Then Sister Patsy grasped the towel on the wall with both hands, where it was joined to make a loop, and ripped the seam open. She tore off a long narrow strip and folded it into a washcloth, which she held under the tap, now running warm. She rubbed the cloth on a bar of soap that was sitting in a wire holder above the sink and began systematically washing the girl's body, and at the end sluicing her down by squeezing the sopping wet cloth, so that the water ran away and into a drain in the floor.

All the while the girl swayed but kept on her feet, leaning, with her hands on the wall over the basin where Sister Patsy had put her. Now she began to shiver violently. Sister Patsy knelt and removed her wet socks, then took the rest of the towelling and dried her, rubbing the rough cloth vigorously and quickly over her body. Once done, she led the shivering girl to the day-bed and, with gestures that were quick and efficient but possessed now a palpable tenderness, pushed the clothes on to the floor, laid the girl on the back half of the chenille bed-cover, put a cushion under her head, turned the front of the cover over the girl's body, and got an old wool blanket from the cupboard and put this over her as well. Finally, she got a chipped, heavy tumbler from a shelf in the cupboard, filled it with warm water, and made the girl drink it.

After looking to see that the girl's shivering had subsided, and that she might sleep, Sister Patsy collected the scattered clothes and folded them on top of the cupboard. Then she got some cleaning rags from the bottom of the cupboard and a mop and bucket and set to work on the toilet and the floor. A pair of filthy underpants she found in a corner she flushed down the toilet. After wiping out the basin with the torn towelling, she threw it into the cupboard with the cleaning things. She laid the wet socks over a radiator at the foot of the day-bed. Then she got a fresh hand towel and put it on the rod.

A ring with a latchkey and a medallion from a penny arcade had fallen from the girl's trousers. The medallion was stamped around the edge with a name and address, Jacky Mills—4901 Fort Hamilton Parkway. Sister Patsy put the ring and the rest of it on top of the clothes.

So far Sister Patsy had not actually thought about the meaning of any of this. She had done what she had done in a possessed state, with no thought of any kind. Neither had she considered her own condition, and only now looked down at her spattered clothes, which were the ones she had intended to wear for the meeting, and that Neen had spent so much time on that morning. She realized she would have to go home to change, and something had to be done about the girl before the meeting, which was two hours away. She had less time than that, as a matter of fact, because shortly the Dickey–Pottses would arrive with their instruments, as would others who came early to pray.

But these practical concerns were not uppermost in her mind. They would be dealt with when they had to be. She walked out through the cloakroom slowly and sat down in the last pew, on the side of the auditorium, and looked once again across the lines of the pews and the motes of dust in the air toward the meagre light from the windows opposite, not really seeing them, but turning over the images that she only now had the leisure to examine.

Sister Patsy knew she was in shock, and her preternatural lucidity of mind a result of it. Lucid she was, however. And at the lucid centre of her consciousness, displacing every other thing, was the body of the girl. She had never seen a body in that state. An unhealthiness amounting to principle. A rebuke to health. The rickety, bowed thighs and protruding thigh sockets, the sparse dusty hair of the prominent pubis, the curved spine and rounded shoulders, pointed shoulder blades like primitive limbs, orange-brown nipples sunk in little flattish breasts stuck uneasily on a rib-cage, covered, as were the girl's legs and back, in bruises in every stage of coloration. Fresh reddish ones. Old yellow and black ones. And over all the green-white colour of ill-nourished, infrequently washed flesh.

She had seen such things in prints, in the Shoemaker's library. Survivors of sieges in old histories. Abandoned drabs in temperance tracts. Exhumed corpses in illustrated lives of the saints and books of martyrs. But those were bodies as light as a thought, things of bone and parchment, represented by lines and dots, imagined artefacts. This body, however, was real and had weight, and a smell like a pond.

Decisions had been made, she realized, without lingering over them or questioning herself in any way about her motives. Those things any ordinary person would do in these circumstances, Sister Patsy knew were not possible for her to do, whatever the consequences might be. She knew she would not call the police. She was not curious about the causes of the things that had happened. She would not ask the girl to explain anything, or restrain her in any way. These decisions had involved no struggle of conscience or considerations of prudence. There could be no turning back. Indeed, these events, the aborted break-in and the extraordinary presence of the sick girl, and that this strange girl was now lying naked on the day-bed at the back of the church, had not only interrupted the train of thought which had occupied Sister Patsy when she heard the cup breaking in the kitchen. They had transformed everything. Something fundamental had shifted. This girl was a messenger, a gift from the light, an emblem for her in her war with unseen opponents.

Sister Patsy had ceased altogether to think about what she would say at the meeting, and was relieved to hear a vigorous thumping on the outer door, signalling, she had no doubt, the arrival of the Dickey–Potts trio with their instruments.

She unlocked one side of the big front door, then pulled

the bolts, top and bottom, on the other half and opened both doors wide.

"Praise the Lord, Sister," said Velma Dickey, who was angling the vibraphone toward the door of the church, while her sister handed instrument cases from the back door of the bus to Eunice Potts to stack on the sidewalk.

"Well don't you look awful," Velma said, when she got the vibraphone up to the door and managed to look up at Sister Patsy.

"Never mind that," said Sister Patsy, "There's a sick girl on the couch in the toilet. Don't disturb her. But look in on her, will you? I'll be back."

Sister Patsy started to walk away, then came back. "Listen Velma," she said, standing very close and saying it quietly so the others couldn't hear. They both realized that Sister Patsy had never called her by her name like that before, but always said Sister Dickey. "Something is happening, and I'm not sure what. If I'm not back by the time meeting starts, you start without me. Maybe you can get that girl up before people start coming. Her clothes are in there. But don't let her get away. Promise me, Velma."

"I sure will, Sister Shoemaker," said Velma, awed. Then added as Sister Patsy was about to turn away, "It's just as well you're going back home. Neen is in a state. A brother from the church came looking for you about an hour ago, and talked to Neen at the door. We was getting ready and all, so we didn't hear it, but Neen said that woman from the church that was up at your place when we drove up is making trouble, like Neen said she would. Neen is scared."

# 3

"Brother Bringsrud was here," Neen said without any preface.

"I heard from the Dickeys," Sister Patsy said. "What did he want?"

Neen did not at first reply. Sister Patsy turned to the wall to look for something else to wear. She took down a white dress that needed no collar and threw it on the bed. She kicked off her shoes and undid her garters, and slid the dirty stockings off and threw them down.

"Are you curious about why I'm back? Or how I got these things filthy?"

"I told you to watch out for that woman."

"I suppose you are going to tell me eventually what this is all about."

"She told him we was unnatural."

Sister Patsy had pulled her dress off over her head and didn't hear the last words.

"What did you say?"

"We was unnatural. She said we was unnatural."

Sister Patsy went into the bathroom and turned on the tap

in the basin. When it ran hot she put a plug in the drain. She splashed her face with the water and patted herself dry with a towel. Then she dipped a cloth in the water, wrung it out, and wiped her arms and then her legs, putting each foot in turn on the ledge of the tub. She stopped and looked at herself in the mirror over the basin.

Only then did she look up at Neen, who was standing in the door of the bathroom.

"You'll be all right. Things is happening that got nothing to do with you." Sister Patsy softened her tone, but it was not enough.

"What you mean, I'll be all right? What you mean, Got nothing to do with me?"

Neen's voice rose.

"You'll have to leave here. They'll make you leave. I won't be able to be with you."

Sister Patsy pushed past Neen and went back to the bedroom to get the dress she had laid out.

Neen followed her.

"I ain't got no calling or no gift. The Lord sent you to me. I got nothing else."

*Run, Patsy. Run,* the voice from the fog said.

So close it was. Sister Patsy reeled. She caught herself by the head of the bed closest to her, which was Neen's. The essence of Neen's body rose from the bedclothes and mingled with the smell of anxiety from Neen herself, now staring and rigid, and the smells of dust and clothes and shoes and old furniture. And laced through these something scorched, and some thrown-out food, and an antiseptic smell, and something from the stairs, a dry smell of mouldy wallpaper-paste and carpet.

*Run, Patsy. Run.*

Nausea swept over Sister Patsy. It was over. All of this was over. She looked at Neen as though she had never seen her before. Something was in motion in which they were all in great danger. She could not stop here. She could not descend into this now. Neen was retching from the strain, bent and twisted strangely. Sister Patsy had to get away. Now.

*Run, Patsy. Run.*

"In twenty minutes I got to be walking through the church door," Sister Patsy said, and began pulling on the white dress. "Get me a glass of water, and find me some clean shoes and stockings."

When Sister Patsy got back to Ebenezer the service had already begun. The congregation could be heard singing from the sidewalk as soon as she passed the White Tower hamburgers.

*Years I spent in va-ni-ty and pride,*
*Car-ing not my Lord was cru-ci-fied,*
*Know-ing not it was for me He died,*
*At Cal-va-ry.*

She paused to listen beneath the light bulb over the door. The light of the late summer evening was fading. A wind had blown up from the harbour, and far away over New Jersey the sky flashed in warning of an approaching storm. Sister Patsy had brought a shawl against the evening air, and now pulled it tightly around her shoulders.

*Mer-cy there was great and grace was free,*
*Par-don there was mul-ti-plied to me,*
*There my bur-dened soul found vic-to-ry,*
*At Cal-va-ry.*

On the last note of the refrain, before the second stanza began, Sister Patsy opened the door and entered what would be her last meeting at Ebenezer.

# 4

The auditorium is full, fuller than Sister Patsy has ever seen it. There are people from Elim who have forsaken the tent meeting to hear the Dickey–Potts Trio. There are others Sister Patsy recognizes from churches far afield, and many strangers.

Eunice Potts is leading the singing with great sweeps of her arms. On the right-hand side of the platform, Velma is playing the accordion and her sister Loreen the vibraphone, making extra arpeggios and other fancy passages. Over at the piano, Mary Colavito runs rapid octave scales with her right hand and thunderous bass chords with her left. People are enjoying this friendly rivalry, and smile to themselves, and sing ever more lustily the many stanzas and repeated refrains, holding the notes of the final cadence extra long when Eunice Potts lifts her arms high, meaning she wants them to slow down.

*O, the love that drew sal-va-tion's plan,*
*O, the grace that brought it down to man.*

Sister Patsy considers, and then walks slowly down the left aisle. Stopping now and then, careful to move against the beat of the music, touching this one and that one, without looking at them, as though she knows them by touch alone and also needs their strength in order to continue. Feathered hats turn. Necks in starched collars crane. Features soften.

*O, the migh-ty gulf that God did span,*
*At Cal-va-ry.*

Reaching the platform, Sister Patsy paces slowly, with many pauses, the length and breadth of her carpet, her fine nose sniffing the atmosphere. She stands briefly with her back to the congregation. She walks to the piano and looks absently into its mechanism. She returns to the front of the platform and looks past Eunice Potts's waving arms, over the heads and into the pews and into the earth beneath the floor.

She is like a captain, feeling his ship beneath him. The cargo and the passengers are safest when he is not thinking of them or their safety, but when every nerve is attuned to the draught and the tack, the drag of the tide, reading by honed instinct the hum of the lines and the creak of the bottom. The ship is this moment, her life, which she feels now as a thing of delicate and dangerous motions. She has come to rest on her favourite spot, directly over the horrible baptismal tank, that tank of bilge and dread, which is also a resonator below her, amplifying the music, turning it into pure vibration which she feels in her knees and around her hips beneath the white dress, and makes the dress itself feel everywhere on her an irritation, a weight, without which she would float free as air.

*Mer-cy there was great and grace was free.*

Ole Knudsen is sitting down near the front, his arm along the back of the pew behind Florence Hagen, his fingers touching her bare upper arm. Ragnar Sivertsen is near them, sitting alone, looking from time to time over to the side, where Neen usually sits. Brother Bringsrud is in the middle, toward the back, his forehead knit with worry, looking, she thinks, like a first mate who thinks the topsails should be reefed. Sister Patsy sends a faint smile directly at him, which increases his frown and brings colour to his face. To her right, near the piano, are Sister Agnes and Sister Sara. Their open faces and broad shoulders and the sceptical way they look at the Dickey–Potts Trio make her want to laugh.

*Par-don there was mul-ti-plied to me.*

Sister Patsy walks to her left, in front of the Dickey sisters, the various instruments they will use during the service displayed around them. She looks full in Velma Dickey's face, round and gleaming above the jerking pleats of the accordion, her crimped hair rising above her forehead in a pyramid. She searches there momentarily, and learns from certain shifts of Velma's eyes in the direction of the ladies' toilet, and then towards the door, and a wobble of her chin upwards, that the girl had been moved and was not in the church.

Sister Patsy picks up something else. A warning perhaps.

*There my bur-dened soul found vic-to-ry—*

Sister Patsy considers for a moment, her eyes shut. She descends from the platform and crosses the empty space to the first pew, and leaning across it, says something to a startled Ragnar Sivertsen, who flushes, and then looks serious, and gets up, excusing himself to Florence Hagen and Ole Knudsen as he slides past them, and strides, with head down, toward the door beneath the clock.

Sister Patsy returns to the platform. Every eye is devouring her, absorbing her every move.

*At C-a-l-l-l-v-a-a-r-y-y-y.*

The service goes forward smoothly. The Dickey–Potts Trio sing and play two special numbers. In between the two special numbers Eunice Potts gives her testimony, which is shy and awkward and makes people murmur with sympathy and approval. After, there is another congregational song. And then a general season of prayer and thanksgiving, in which the older Norwegians turn and kneel in the pews. Others lift their hands and wave them. Some take out handkerchiefs and blow into them. After this there is another special from the Dickey–Potts Trio and Loreen gives her testimony, how the Lord saved her. Then a more jokey sort of special, with funny noises from Eunice Potts's trombone and more fancy work from Velma's accordion, and Loreen on the Hammond organ sounding like a train leaving a station and accelerating down the track, which puts everyone in the mood for Velma's testimony, for which she is well known, and has everyone saying Praise the Lord and laughing and wiping tears from their eyes.

Then they do a more serious number, which has a favourite refrain that the congregation join in, and leads to yet others that they know well and sing with their eyes shut. Everyone is invited to stand and sing some more, which leads to more praying and waving hands about, while the older Norwegians turn and kneel again.

After this rich feast it is not expected that Sister Patsy will preach a long sermon. Nevertheless, there is a hush of expectancy, which deepens as Sister Patsy rises from the chair she has occupied at the back edge of the platform. She stands alone and straight, her arms hanging by her side, her slender wrists pale and motionless, and waits.

In the stillness thunder can be heard from the harbour, mingled with the flat rumble and faint sigh of the Fourth Avenue Local pulling in to the 53rd Street subway station on the corner, and the light patter of rain on the windows high up on the wall and on the flat tar-paper roof. The air grows cool. Still Sister Patsy waits.

"Do you know the Lord?"

Not everyone hears the words. They aren't expecting them just then. So conversational they are, and unremarkable. People strain forward in their seats, and cock their heads slightly to one side.

"Do you know the Lord?"

A gust of wind rattles rain onto the tar paper roof like loose gravel.

"Have you seen him?"

There is a flash in the windows behind the piano. People turn their heads. Brother Bringsrud's lips move as he counts the seconds . . . *four, five.* Then a distant roll of thunder.

"Have you seen him?"

Brows in the congregation furrow gradually as though at an impertinence that has only dawned.

"He was bruised for our i-ni-qui-ty," says Sister Patsy with tremendous intensity.

Florence Hagen shivers and shakes her hair and moves her shoulders away from Ole Knudsen's arm. Ole has become acutely conscious of Florence's smell, which is of clean sweat and oranges and starched cotton, of brushed hair and face powder, and something deeper as well, none of which is diminished in its effect by the smells of varnish from the pews and hot electric bulbs in the fixtures on the low ceiling of Ebenezer. Ole Knudsen discovers he is in love with Florence Hagen and resolves to ask her to marry him.

"Say it with me."

Sister Patsy pronounces it slowly and with exaggeration. "B-b-r-o-o-o-z-z-d."

Sister Sara, called Sara-with-the-hat-on, had shut her eyes as soon as Sister Patsy began, and is now rocking ever so slightly, backwards and forwards, and nods her head each time Sister Patsy speaks.

"H-n-n-n," she says softly.

Here and there other sisters do the same.

"H-n-n-n," comes softly from Happy Olsen, and from the woman with a face like a cat.

"H-n-n-n."

And old Sister Norli, who was a missionary in China, and whose face is pitted from smallpox.

"H-n-n-n."

These are the three aristocrats of suffering in Ebenezer. They are poor, and wear dark cloth coats all year round and sad, crushed hats, like a uniform.

"B-b-r-o-o-o-z-z-d."

Sister Patsy says the word again, yet more slowly, as one teaching a child a new word, or a foreigner a new language.

"Take your time. It is difficult," she says.

People look at one another furtively. Some begin to purse their lips, not sure whether or not to repeat it after her.

"B-b-r-o-o-o-z-z-d," she says again.

A tentative buzzing murmur comes from the crowd, which might be "bruised," and might not. Sister Patsy treats this as a promising beginning, with the air of a school mistress encouraging well-behaved but dull pupils.

"B-b-r-o-o-o-z-z-d," they manage.

Sister Patsy raises her eyebrows.

"B-b-r-o-o-o-z-z-d," she says.

"B-b-r-o-o-o-z-z-d," comes back again.

Smiles appear on faces. They do it again. Now Sister Patsy

only has to lift her hand and a wail lifts from two hundred voices, even the children in the front pews.

"B-b-r-o-o-o-z-z-d," they all sing, now without prompting, marvelling at the trick, reducing the word to nonsense, defeating its authority, feeling it in the mouth as a tickle of the lips, a slide, a tickle on the tips of the teeth.

"B-b-r-o-o-o-z-z-d."

Sister Patsy lifts both her hands, palms outward, and they stop obediently.

"Now shut your eyes, dear brothers and sisters. Everyone. I see you there. Shut your eyes. Yes, you too. All the boys and girls down in the front. Mother and father. Man and woman. Young and old. Whatever your burden tonight. Whomever you love. Whatever you serve. Shut your eyes."

Her voice is soft and has a nervous flutter that catches the heart. Every spirit is subdued. Every mind is quiet. Into this quiet Sister Patsy's breath moves, as does the wind that flutters the aspen leaf when every other leaf is still. And this is the fragment that Sister Patsy speaks that night, carefully, with many pauses, not hesitatingly, but so that the dullest may keep up with her. Gently, in Ebenezer, in the quiet, except for the rain and the distant thunder, with everyone's eyes shut.

"Imagine this—" she says.

# 5

"A man goes down from Jerusalem to Jericho and is set upon by thieves, who rob him and beat him and leave him naked and wounded and near to death by the side of the road.

"Already you know the rest of this story. Yes, you know it. You have heard this story. You do not need me to tell it to you. I will continue anyway. You may have missed something. I may miss something. I will try to tell you this story that you have already heard.

"The Priest and the Levite look at this naked man, and walk by, on the other side of the road.

"A Samaritan comes too. He stops, and anoints and binds the wounds of the traveller and takes him to an inn and pays for his recovery with two pennies, and with his two pennies has earned his place in the Bible as the Good Samaritan.

"Ah! You have run on ahead of me. You are cleverer than me. You are at the end while I am still at the beginning. I have nothing to tell you about this story that you don't know. I should run ahead to something new, something you haven't heard. But I have to linger here. I cannot leave the story.

"I am not so clever as others who have heard this story. I am not good enough to grasp it at once. I cannot understand this Good Samaritan so easily. I cannot even get to that part of the story where he becomes the Good Samaritan. This man that always knows what to do. That always has the right money in his pocket when it comes to pay for something. Who knows the ways of landlords and innkeepers. And has such a lot of business he must be off and will come back later. And knows about oils and lotions and mending injured bodies. Maybe you know such people. I don't know such people. I cannot think about it. I will be in despair.

"Can the Priest and the Levite make me feel any better? No, I am defeated here as well. I know I am supposed to hate and despise them. But I cannot even lift my head in their presence. These people who size things up. Who decide what is best. Who have projects on their minds, and destinations. Who weigh the particular and the general the way I decide on apples and pears. Who have obligations to their families and their kin. To their callings and their traditions. Who am I to say anything about such people.

"No, I am still on that road from Jerusalem to Jericho. In my weakness and diseased imaginings. I am there before any of them comes along. I wonder about this man lying there. But I wonder to no purpose. There is nothing to know, except this disaster which has come upon him like a sudden storm. His character, his past, his future, are all hidden. He is beaten, he is stripped, he is left half dead.

"The story is specific on one point. The Priest and the Levite saw him. They looked at him.

"That I understand. That is where, in my simplicity, I stop. I can go no further. I too look. My eyes start out of my head at the sight.

"Fists. Knees and feet. Sticks. Unknown assailants have bruised his flesh and broken his bones. Blood comes from his mouth and nose. Great bruises appear around his ribs and across his shoulders. Welts lie like stripes on his thighs. His feet are broken and his arms lie at crazy angles. His hair is caked with filth, and his private parts are exposed, so that he would be shamed before his children and his household were they to see him. It is a mercy that only strangers see him.

"I am a stranger. I should not be looking. I should move on. I should do something. Maybe I should cover him up. Say a few words. But I am mute, aghast, paralysed, rooted to the spot. I am useless. I see no meaning in this.

"Then in my sinfulness I grow tired of shock and grief. I become curious. I inch forward and look at the colours of his bruises, the strange dent in the side of his skull. I see that his feet were dirty from the road, that his hand was calloused from work, that the sun had burnt his cheek. I memorize these details so I can repeat them when I am asked, or when I am lonely and want to think on the events of my life and what I have seen in my journeys.

"Then I say to myself that I will embroider this story. Who will contradict me?

"I will say that I saw the attack on him. That I did what I could to defend him. I will say that he was already dead when I found him.

"I will say that I knew of him. That he was a seducer of innocence, beaten in revenge by the kinsmen of his victim. That he was a usurer, an unjust landlord, a rapacious and cruel collector of debts, getting the proper punishment from those he has wronged. A thief himself, it may be, fallen out with thieves—

"But it is time to awake from my dreams and my fantasies.

"Open your eyes everyone, and look at me."

The congregation obey, as Sister Patsy continues.

"For is this not a parable? A tale told by our Lord himself? What right do I have to stop in this story and make things up?

"It is a mystery, this story. Did our Lord thus speak, in figures, of his own sufferings? His bruised and broken body, which was bruised before the beginning of the world? That no earthly power can mend?

"Did He not know that I was weak, and could only stare, until my eye sockets became hollow and dry? Did He not know that I would betray Him? That I would make things up? Twist the facts this way and that? Is that why he was bruised? That I would know this?

"I cannot even fall on my face and repent. My shame is foretold. It was fixed already from the beginning of the story. Where I would have to stop, in shame and defeat. The story has a great pit in the centre of it, an abyss.

"Beware. Beware of this bruised and naked body. To look upon it is to know thyself.

"Do you see? Do you dare to look?"

Sister Patsy paused at this point in her narration, in which her voice had never risen or her attitude altered from when she had begun. It was not clear whether she intended to go on, or was able to go on. Mary Colavito slid onto the piano seat, from her place against the wall, prepared to play softly for the altar call which usually followed the sermon, although she was aware of the strangeness of what she had heard, and hesitated.

In that moment, someone opened the inner door from the street, the door that had the clock above it that said Redeem the Time. Every head turned to see.

Ragnar Sivertsen stood there, his hair wet. He was panting. He had been running. It took Sister Patsy a moment to remember that she had sent him to check on Neen.

He motioned to Sister Patsy to come to him and then he stepped back through the door into the vestibule.

Sister Patsy put her hand to her mouth. In that moment it came to her with devastating force. Nathalie Thornquist was not in the meeting.

How could she have been so stupid? How could she have let her guard down, not to notice? She guessed what had happened. They had taken the girl to Mary Colavito's place. It was the only place they could have taken her. And Nathalie Thornquist had gone there and made trouble, and dragged Neen into it.

Instead of going directly to Ragnar Sivertsen, Sister Patsy walked to the piano.

"What happened to that girl, Mary?" she said quietly, her face shielded from the congregation by the upturned piano lid, and trying to keep her voice under control.

"Sister Dickey said they needed to do something about a girl that was sick," Mary whispered, "They said it was for you. I said she could stay with me. My roommate is away—"

Sister Patsy interrupted, "Never mind that. How did she get there?"

"I saw Sister Thornquist come in and I asked if we could use her car, and she said she would take her, and I gave her the key. Sister Dickey got her dressed— What's the matter?"

"Come with me."

Sister Patsy dragged Mary Colavito behind her down the aisle, Mary stumbling in her built-up shoe. There were now murmurs of disbelief from the congregation, who were still sitting, except for Brother Bringsrud, who was standing in his place stunned. He looked beseechingly at Sister Patsy and caught her eye. But she had a distant, faraway look, as one who is already a stranger. On the platform Velma Dickey was saying something, and then began playing the accordion to get the congregation singing.

When at last Sister Patsy reached Ragnar Sivertsen in the vestibule, he was staring and silent. There was a policeman with him.

"Well?" Sister Patsy said.

"Neen is dead," said Ragnar Sivertsen.

# 6

Miss Sparrow had smelled gas, and let herself in to the upstairs flat to investigate. The kitchen was shut up tight, and when she forced the door open and looked in she saw Neen slumped with her head in the oven. She had held her breath, she explained to the police and the ambulance driver, all she could do was turn off the gas and get herself out again, and down to her own flat and phone the operator.

They brought Neen to the emergency at Norwegian Hospital, but it was too late.

Sister Patsy took this all in without interrupting, in the vestibule by the steps. Then the policeman said, when Ragnar was done, that the detective wanted somebody to come and answer some questions and help them look for a note maybe. And somebody close to her would have to go to the hospital and identify the body.

"You go along with Ragnar," Sister Patsy said to Mary Colavito, "and see what you can do. They'll let you look through her things. I don't think you'll find any note."

Mary Colavito stared back at her. "Sure, I—" she began,

tears starting out in her eyes with love and pride that Sister Patsy had appointed her in her own stead.

"Go on, then," Sister Patsy said, with grave patience, and kissed Mary Colavito on each of her wet eyes. "I got things to do that won't keep."

The policeman opened the outer door. Rain was coming down hard, slanting through the light from the single bulb shining above.

Sister Patsy spoke to Ragnar. "When you're done with the police, take Mary home. There's a girl there. Mary will explain. You watch over them 'til I get there. I'll come later."

Ragnar nodded.

"Where you going? You all right?" Mary Colavito said, with the courage of her new responsibility.

Sister Patsy smiled gently. "I got to arrange something for the Dickey–Pottses." She waved her hand to indicate other things. "I got to go see Neen."

She pushed them out the door and heard them scurry to the protection of the awning at the White Tower. She shut the door against the rain and stood for a moment alone in the vestibule, breathing slowly and deeply. From inside she heard someone playing the piano, and Eunice Potts's young bass voice leading the congregation.

*Spi-rit, now melt and move—*

She pushed open the inner door, slipped inside and went down to the front. Velma Dickey came to the front of the platform and Sister Patsy spoke in her ear. Then Sister Patsy turned and caught Brother Bringsrud's eye, and also Sister Sara's.

*All of our hearts with love.*

Sister Patsy started toward the back again, toward the cloakroom, drawing Velma Dickey and Brother Bringsrud and Sister Sara after her, and, on an impulse, stopped and spoke briefly to Florence Hagen, who followed the others.

When they had assembled in the cloakroom next to the ladies' toilet, Sister Patsy told Brother Bringsrud and Sister Sara, Florence Hagen and Velma Dickey, that Neen was dead and that she was leaving Ebenezer, and that once she left—which was now, in just a moment—she would never be back.

The singing of the congregation could be heard through the door.

*Breathe on us from a-bove—*

Brother Bringsrud looked up sharply, and started to open his mouth, but shut it again and looked down at his feet. Sister Sara wept.

*With o-o-ld ti-i-me pow'r.*

Sister Patsy said that the Dickey–Potts Trio could not stay in her place after what happened and would Florence Hagen find room for them at her house. Ole could help get their things out of the flat. She expected the Dickey–Pottses would finish out the revival meetings. She, Sister Patsy, would need nothing.

Florence Hagen agreed to see that the Dickey–Pottses got everything moved to her place. She reached out to touch Sister Patsy but was inhibited by Sister Patsy's remote dignity, and let her hand fall.

There was no rancour in Sister Patsy's voice as she spoke to them in the cloakroom, with the smell of varnish and disinfectant in their noses, just standing as they had come in, awkwardly standing around, with no tables or chairs or papers or formality. She had said no more than what she had needed to say. She betrayed to them nothing about the rumours that she realized were already circulating, the work of Nathalie Thornquist.

These rumours were the reason, and not the Dickey–Pottses, for the big turn-out tonight, in spite of the Elim tent meeting. She knew also, with detached and bitter irony, that Neen's death would insure a good attendance for the rest of the revival.

They came out of the cloakroom, Sister Patsy first. Sister Patsy had put on an old raincoat she kept there, and was carrying a man's large umbrella.

Every head was now turned, ignoring Eunice Potts's arm-waving. Velma Dickey walked to the platform, the others remained in a knot at the back.

As Sister Patsy left she heard Velma Dickey speaking, and then a shocked exhalation.

# 7

All of this had taken very little time, but Sister Patsy was now mad with regret for every minute. Alone in the wet streets, she cursed her dilatoriness and stupidity. Her stride grew long, wearing down the pain in her hip and the stitch in her side, on the steep hill, on the broken and tilted and slippery slates under the trees.

At Fifth Avenue she turned left into the lights. Shoppers and strollers in light summer clothing sheltered in shop doorways, waiting for the rain to stop. Others dashed here and there with newspapers on their heads. The Italian fruit stall man on 52nd Street was pulling some of his wares back under his awning. Up and down the avenue, the neon beer signs of the saloons whispered among the garish lights of the furniture and pawn shops.

Sister Patsy set herself on a diagonal course across the avenue, darting between parked cars and across the trolley tracks. Her white shoes got soaked in the puddles and slid on the glazed paving blocks. She turned at 49th Street, for no other reason than that it was the steepest block in her path.

She felt the need of opposition, of difficulty, to brace her for what was to come.

A garter clasp came loose. Without breaking her stride she loosened the others, which released the weight of her stockings on her hips and made her movements easier. At the top of the hill, on Sixth Avenue, the rain stopped. Sister Patsy furled her umbrella, and pulled her stockings off, leaning on an iron paling with a privet hedge behind it. She shoved the stockings in her raincoat pocket, stepped into her wet shoes again and turned left on Sixth Avenue, which now ran level toward the entrance to the park. She met no one, and flew quickly past the churches and white terrace-houses that lined the avenue.

On the corner by the entrance to the park where, only the night before, the Friends from Ebenezer had held their street meeting, stood a compact apartment building of four stories, with ornate stone details around the windows and fake balconies in wrought iron.

Sister Patsy went to the entrance around the corner on 45th Street. There was a double row of buttons at the side with names next to each one. She found what she was looking for. N. Thornquist, Apt. 4B.

She pressed the big lever handle. The door was locked. She peered through the door into a dimly lit lobby. Most of the far wall was covered by a mirror in which she could see herself on the other side of the iron grillwork and heavy glass. She hesitated for a moment, and then went back around the corner of the building to the Sixth Avenue side, to a narrow opening in the basement.

Three steps down, and a passageway through to the back of the building. She tried the doors along the passageway, feeling for them in the dark, with no success. She came out at the back in a little cement courtyard and looked up at the fire escape, but realized she could not get to the dangling iron ladder, mounted up out of reach.

She returned to the sidewalk and began to go around the corner again, when she saw someone coming out of the building. To her relief, whoever it was turned away from her without looking around and walked down the hill. The door was closing slowly, and she reached it just before it clicked shut.

Once inside, Sister Patsy stepped into an alcove where the tenants' mailboxes were located, and listened. A door opened high up inside. There was a distant sound of feet on stairs. A heavy tread, mounting. A faint click, as of a bolt. Then a scraping sound. And a draught of cooler air.

She took off her shoes and, carrying them in one hand, and the umbrella in the other, ran barefoot up the stairs in swift, silent spurts, pausing at each floor and at the landings in between to listen. A radio was playing. Then water running. The smell of a dinner.

At the landing just before the top floor she paused. Her eyes were at a level with the bottom of the doors. The door to 4B was half open. To the right of it another flight of stairs, steeper and narrower, led to a painted metal door, which also stood open, and through it Sister Patsy could see, as she drew up to the foot of the stairs, the night sky and the outline of a vent with a round top whirling and squeaking in the wind.

Sister Patsy put down her shoes and the umbrella on the floor, and with a glance at the roof door above, entered 4B, sliding around the door without moving it.

She was in a small hall with a stand, and a copper bowl on the stand, and a picture on the wall, and an amber light in the ceiling, which was on. Another door led to a sitting room, which was dark, illuminated only by the dim light from the hall, and stuffed with upholstered furniture. The smell of an elderly lap dog made her gag. She feared she was going to be sick.

Her eyes roamed over the little room quickly. On the floor next to the stand there was a cream-coloured leather handbag with a gold clasp. Sister Patsy picked it up and opened it. There, in a centre compartment, closed with a zipper, was what she expected to find.

There was little reason now for caution or stealth. Sister Patsy returned the thing to the bag, but didn't close it. She pulled the door wide and stepped out of the apartment. She put on her shoes, and took the umbrella in her hand, and climbed the stairs.

Sister Patsy stepped out on the roof and stood for a moment

taking in the view, fighting back her fear of the height and the closeness of the edge. Below her lay the park, strings of street lamps marking the paths. The rain had moved to the east, over Borough Park and Flatbush, where the sky was pitch black. Out over the harbour an electrical storm was still flashing high in the atmosphere, lightning streaking across vast distances, illuminating the scurrying clouds far away over the harbour, lighting up the skyscrapers of Manhattan. A line of tanks and derricks crouched low on the horizon in New Jersey.

She could see the Empire State Building and its radio tower etched on the night.

"You have come looking for me, I see."

The voice was behind her, over her left shoulder.

Sister Patsy didn't turn immediately, but continued looking out over the city and the harbour. She could hear thunder in the sky directly above them.

"You are missing something, are you?" the voice said. "You have come to beg me, of course, beg that I will not say anything. You may as well know that your tricks will not work on me. It is too late for that anyway. The filthiness will be exposed."

Sister Patsy turned to look at Nathalie Thornquist, who was busy with something as she spoke. When Sister Patsy's eyes adjusted to the darkness of the roof after the brilliance of the view over the city, she saw that the woman was hanging something to air, on a wire strung between the hatch and a metal pole. It was the string of furs with little bead eyes Nathalie Thornquist had worn earlier.

Sister Patsy lunged forward and snatched the thing away from Nathalie Thornquist. She sniffed it. She gripped the thing in both her hands. She pressed her nose into it.

She sniffed it again.

"You were there!"

Sister Patsy had no more strength in her. She dropped the fur and sank to her knees on the wet tar of the roof, overcome with grief and remorse.

"It was you destroyed her," said Nathalie Thornquist in the mechanical voice of a ventriloquist. "You and your filthiness. I brought her the evidence. You thought it was hidden, your filthiness. But the Lord led me to it."

Nathalie Thornquist's voice rose.

"Right into the church you brought it. Nakedness and filth and unnatural lusts. A decent girl isn't enough. Cripples. And whores from the street. I showed her that picture. I told her you had a girl right in the church."

She was now out of control, and began to kick Sister Patsy where she knelt on the tar of the roof.

"Pretty ways!" Her voice minced in mockery. "Pretty dresses! Little shoes on our little feet! A mockery in the House of the Lord! Men and women, either one, no doubt! Unnatural! Unnatural!"

With each phrase she gave Sister Patsy another kick. Sister

Patsy tried to avoid her as the pain stabbed her ribs and her hip, and she was driven back against the hatch by the door.

"That girl was snatched from the burning . . . She is in a better place . . . You destroyed that girl's spiritual gift with filthiness . . . She saw it all before the Lord took her to himself . . . The Lord made me an instrument."

Sister Patsy was now on all fours, trying to rise. She crawled and stumbled into the middle of the roof, where she at last managed to sit up against the low parapet around an air well.

Nathalie Thornquist had to pause. Her breath came in short gasps. She had picked up the umbrella Sister Patsy had dropped near the door. She lifted it menacingly.

"I saw you for what you were, right from the beginning. I have a gift of discernment from the Holy Ghost—"

"DAMN THE HOLY GHOST!" shrieked Sister Patsy, and shut her eyes and slumped forward with her hands over her head, waiting for the blow.

# 8

The blow she was expecting never came. Sister Patsy only remembered afterwards a sudden pain in her ears, and then a numbness and ringing, and that a fierce light penetrated her shut eyelids and left a blue image on her retina for many seconds.

When she was able to open her eyes and see clearly again, Nathalie Thornquist had disappeared. She could smell ozone and burning in the air, and heard distant thunder, and felt rain coming down. She pulled herself up to the parapet and looked over.

A square of light at the bottom of the air well, from a window in the lobby, showed part of the sprawled form of Nathalie Thornquist.

Sister Patsy sat down again and shut her eyes and waited and listened.

She opened one eye, and then the other. There was no commotion in the building. No one had heard Nathalie Thornquist fall. The crash of lightning and thunder must have covered the sound. She picked up the umbrella, found her shoes and started to put them on. Then she thought better of it and held them in her hand. She descended the stairs through the open door and arrived again in front of the open door to Nathalie Thornquist's flat.

Sister Patsy stepped inside for the second time that night, and pulled the door quietly shut.

She went to the bathroom and turned on the light. She washed her face with a washcloth, and straightened her hair with a comb she found in a cupboard. She flushed the hair that got pulled out in the comb down the toilet and washed the comb before returning it to the cupboard. She washed her legs and feet with the washcloth, took her stockings out of her coat pocket and pulled them on and fastened the garters. She winced from the bruises on her body, but nothing showed, and nothing seemed to be broken.

She cleaned her raincoat and shoes as best she could with the washcloth, and swished it around the floor to remove any wet marks, before rinsing it and hanging it on the edge of the tub.

Suddenly conscious how hungry and thirsty she was, she went to the kitchen and got a glass of water. She tried to eat a slice of white bread she found in the bread box but couldn't swallow it, and spit it out into the sink and washed it down the drain.

She went back into the entrance hall and got Nathalie Thornquist's handbag and took out the picture with Mary

Colavito in it. She went to the kitchen and hunted until she found a pair of scissors. On the kitchen table she carefully cut out two squares from the photograph.

The larger one showed just the man and the woman. Mary Colavito's hand showed, where it was touching the woman, but not her deformed foot. Sister Patsy was satisfied that Mary would never be identified from the hand alone. She also cut away the margins of the photograph, to make it impossible to guess what its original dimensions were. The other, much smaller piece, showed Mary Colavito's head and shoulders with leaves in her hair. Sister Patsy put this in her pocket.

She burned all the scraps on the top of the gas stove, one piece at a time, and washed the ashes down the drain in the sink. Then she took the larger piece she had cut out and put it in Nathalie Thornquist's handbag, in the centre section with the zipper. She closed the gold clasp, and set the bag on the floor where she had found it.

As she was about to shut the door of the apartment behind her, she glanced into the dark, overstuffed living room and was arrested by a glint of eyes.

An elderly spaniel, lying on a cushion in the centre of the sofa, was looking directly at her.

Sister Patsy stopped. She stepped back inside and picked up Nathalie Thornquist's bag. She opened it and took out the picture she had planted, and put it in her pocket with the picture of Mary Colavito.

Enough is enough.

Sister Patsy went out again, shutting the door firmly without looking back, and turned her mind to poor, tormented Neen, dead at Norwegian Hospital.

# 9

At the hospital they showed her Neen's body in a chilly room. She signed a paper that it was Neen, except it said on the paper Naomi Wilhide, which was Neen's real name, and that she had no kin living close by and Sister Patsy was the closest to her. There would be a post-mortem examination, they said, and then Sister Patsy could have the body. A policeman offered to take her home, but Sister Patsy said she could walk.

She left the hospital and walked in the direction of Mary Colavito's place on 28th Street. The storm had moved away and was rumbling distantly to the east. Stars were shining over the harbour and over New Jersey. The streets were wet from the rain and reflected the traffic lights all the way down Fourth Avenue. Green, and then red, and then green and red together, all the lights in unison, as far as she could see.

Her way took her past the tower of St. Michael's, its high, narrow white dome shining luminous against the black sky. On an impulse she entered through a side door that stood open, and climbed a short flight of steps to the darkened nave, lit only by banks of candles in iron frames and the red gleam of the oil lamp above the high altar. The muscles in her side and her lower back and along her thighs were now beginning to cramp where she had been kicked and had fallen. Flashes of pain travelled up to her skull. She limped slowly down the side aisle nearest her toward a small chapel where there were many candles burning. When she got there she lit a candle for Neen, and knelt down in front of the heart of Jesus burning in his chest behind the rail. These alien gestures now seemed the most natural thing in the world to her. It occurred to her for the first time how free she was. She owed nothing to anyone any more. Her old life was over.

With that thought came another, the realization of what this freedom had cost. She had decided not to call the police about the girl. She had no defence for this. It had not been in the girl's interest she had done it, or for any abstract principle. In any case it would not have been in her character to act on principles, just because they were principles. She had always acted on instinct. No, she had wanted the girl for herself. Because she needed a sign. Because she imagined herself alone in a war with no weapons. She had decided to leave Neen out of her confidence. She had given in to her impatience with Neen, given in to her disgust. She had left Neen defenceless. It had been a heartless, deliberate abandonment. And now Neen was dead.

Two women were dead tonight. Dead from a choice she had made and could not unmake.

Sister Patsy's hand reached in her pocket and her fingers touched the photographs. She took out the larger one and studied it in the light of the candles. What had she said to Mary Colavito? Never give up something of yourself until you know what it has to teach you? How facile that sounded now. How easy to speak of being taught when others pay the price of your education. She had put people around her at risk. How could anyone know when they had learned something? Or what it was?

She had not seen this image since Mary Colavito brought it to her that day in Camden and lay on the bed sobbing in her coat and hat. Had she been so cold then too? Why had she not cradled the creature in her arms and kissed her and stroked her hair and crooned to her like a mother?

Sister Patsy looked again at the photograph in her hand. Her eyes searched hungrily the body of the woman that filled the centre of the photograph. Enormous it was. Magnificent. She traced with her finger the shadow in the bow of the back, and where the waist drew in below the ribs. Her finger followed the outline of the white, round buttocks that began so high, and swelled, white and full, pushing out, filling space, abundant, beyond guilt, beyond meaning. She ran her fingers lightly over them and lifted them to her lips and gently kissed them. She kissed too the little disembodied hand of Mary Colavito, tiny on that white magnificence. Mary had been there. Her hand had touched it, rested on it, brought it into being. She kissed the dark cleft in that white magnificence, and the dark composite animal suspended there, an improbable architecture of primitive life-forms without hands or arms or eyes or thoughts. She sensed, riding over the incense smell of the church, the smell of a tidal river, of salt and weeds and crabs, of things long dead, and things alive again.

What had she missed in her life? Was it an absence that called to her out of the grey cloud and said *Run, Patsy. Run?* What was it like to be naked with this nakedness? To open so far as this. To open until there was nothing left that was closed. To be filled until there was no empty space anywhere.

The pain came again, sharp at the base of her skull. Her thighs quivered uncontrollably and her back was a great stabbing flame. Sister Patsy's face turned, eyes open but unseeing, to the bleeding heart of Jesus. She opened her mouth wide in a scream with no sound, the tendons in her neck stretched taut. Tears ran down her cheeks. Her bruised body hung on one long intolerable spasm of agony, suspended between unconsciousness and pain, between death and life.

She slumped into the wave. It passed. She could not mourn the dead. She could not repent. Not now. She might walk with mourning and repentance through her waking hours all her days. She would perhaps rise in the morning with them, and in time they might become her familiars. But not now, not yet.

She waited for the fog. It did not come. The voice was silenced. It was over. Sister Patsy was free.

Sister Patsy forced herself to her feet. She held the picture to the flame of the candle she had lit for Neen and watched as the photographic paper curled and the man and the woman turned brown and blistered, and writhed together in a simulacrum of passion a last time before they disappeared forever.

# 10

Mary Colavito's room was in the front part of the ground floor of a tall yellow tenement with wooden siding, set between two empty lots. By the time Sister Patsy got there she was nearly dead from fatigue and pain. Mary led her in and sat her on the edge of her bed. She chased Ragnar Sivertsen away, who had been waiting with her for Sister Patsy.

As soon as Ragnar was gone, Mary Colavito fell on her knees in front of Sister Patsy, not daring to touch her.

"The picture is gone!" she breathed in a hoarse and agonized whisper. "How could it have happened. I've done something terrible, haven't I? It was hidden. There under the paper."

Mary pointed to a drawer yanked out and her things flung about.

"That woman must have looked for it. How did she know? Does this have something to do with Neen?"

At first, Sister Patsy seemed not to hear. She shook herself and looked across the end of the L-shaped room at the other bed and the still form on it.

Mary's eyes followed her gaze. "She woke up once and asked for water," Mary said. "This was in her pocket."

Mary held out to Sister Patsy the key ring with the medallion.

Sister Patsy said, "It's got nothing to do with Neen."

She took Mary's hand.

"Look, Mary, I'm leaving—"

She glanced over at the girl in the other bed.

"I'm leaving," she repeated. "As soon as I can. Tomorrow maybe—"

Mary opened her mouth to say something.

"I can't answer any questions."

Sister Patsy looked searchingly at Mary before continuing.

"I'll leave you some money. Fix up with my landlady about the flat. Somewhere in Neen's things is the name of a sister. She should be buried with her folks. You know about arranging things with the railroad. Pay for it with the money. Sell any of my things you don't want. Any money left over I want you to keep."

She looked again at the sleeping girl. She handed the cheap medallion back to Mary. "Jacky from Fort Hamilton Parkway. See that she gets home, will you?"

Sister Patsy pulled Mary down beside her on the bed. She fished in the pocket of her raincoat. "This is what's left. I burned the rest."

Sister Patsy held between her fingers the small picture, the fragment she had cut out that had just Mary Colavito in her Grecian shift and leaves in her hair.

She spoke gravely and with infinite tenderness.

"Take this, Mary, and put it in a little frame, and when Ragnar asks you to marry him, you will not answer but will give this to him and ask him to keep it. You will tell him everything, leaving nothing out. He will take the picture from you and go away. He will come again and ask you again to marry him, and you will say yes.

"And now I must sleep."

Sister Patsy allowed Mary to strip her clothes from her, and put her in a nightgown that belonged to her roommate. Mary eased Sister Patsy's head on to the pillow and covered her with a sheet. Then she pulled the tattered armchair up between the two beds. She dragged over a small locker and put a cushion on it for a foot rest, and made herself comfortable, and waited for the dawn, her mind filled with the promise that had been made to her.